For Emily & Julia —

POSTCARDS
FROM
VENICE

Adventure awaits!! :)

Dee
Romita ♡

Also by Dee Romito

The BFF Bucket List

Best. Night. Ever.
with coauthors

No Place Like Home

POSTCARDS FROM VENICE

DEE ROMITO

Aladdin MIX
New York   London   Toronto   Sydney   New Delhi

ALADDIN M!X

Simon & Schuster Children's Publishing Division

1230 Avenue of the Americas, New York, New York 10020

First Aladdin M!X edition May 2018

Text copyright © 2018 by Deanna Romito

Cover illustration copyright © 2018 by Annabelle Metayer

Also available in an Aladdin hardcover edition.

For information about special discounts for bulk purchases, please contact Simon & Schuster Special Sales at 1-866-506-1949 or business@simonandschuster.com.

The Simon & Schuster Speakers Bureau can bring authors to your live event. For more information or to book an event contact the Simon & Schuster Speakers Bureau at 1-866-248-3049 or visit our website at www.simonspeakers.com.

Cover designed by Nina Simoneaux

Interior designed by Mike Rosamilia

The text of this book was set in Excelsior LT Std.

Manufactured in the United States of America 0418 OFF

2 4 6 8 10 9 7 5 3 1

Library of Congress Control Number 2017959970

ISBN 978-1-5344-0338-3 (hc)

ISBN 978-1-5344-0337-6 (pbk)

ISBN 978-1-5344-0339-0 (eBook)

For my dad, who showed me the world.

And for my husband, Rob, who gave me the world.

ONE

can't wait one more second to see the Floating
City in real life.

Rushing past my mom, I push open the glass
door of the train station.

The pavement and roof make a frame outside
the terminal, surrounding a beautiful panoramic
shot of Venice. It's like I've stepped right into a
painting.

People are everywhere. They're sitting and
standing and pulling suitcases. They're taking
photos and selfies and talking on cell phones.
They're speaking in a million different languages.

I run down the steps and don't stop until I
reach the Grand Canal. Mom finally catches up.

We stand still, not saying a thing. I have no words for what's in front of me.

I'm here.

I'm really here.

There's a stone building with a big green dome taking over the scenery and a big bridge to my left that crosses over the canal. I wonder what's on the other side, behind all the buildings.

Boats of different sizes go by one after another, leaving small waves behind them.

I've spent six incredible days touring Italy with my mom before she starts her new job. And now for the rest of August, we'll be living across the lagoon from Venice while she works.

"We don't have a whole lot of time, Skyler," says Mom. "I do need to get to the office at some point today."

Mom wanted to stay at our new apartment on the mainland and then swing by the office, but not me. No way. I convinced her to take the quick train ride into Venice for some sightseeing first. I've been waiting my whole life to experience this place.

"Can't you start work tomorrow?" I ask. I don't mean it, of course. Six days is already *way* more than Mom has ever taken off work.

She takes out her phone. "I'm sorry, Skyler, but they're expecting me at the office in a bit. We can come into Venice every day for the next four weeks if we want."

I'm not surprised she's dangling this amazing city in front of me only to get started working. I guess I shouldn't expect things to be different right off the bat.

Mom taps her phone screen a few times. "And if this trial period with the company goes well, we can come into Venice every day for the next *year*."

She's right, of course. "Okay, but that bridge is totally calling my name right now," I say. "Plus, Dad's stuck back home while we're here having this grand adventure. I have to send him some pics. So, we can explore a little, right?"

Mom looks at her phone again, but when I give her my puppy dog eyes, she slips it back in her purse.

The first step on the bridge is magical, like I'm entering a new world. Not quite the wardrobe to Narnia or the train to Hogwarts, but close. Seriously close.

I've dreamed of going to Venice since I was a little girl. And here I am, standing in the middle of a bridge, looking out over the Grand Canal. *Officially* in Venice.

"That's a pretty big smile on your face," says Mom. "What do you think?"

I smile even bigger . . . if that's possible. "I love it already," I say. "Like, one million percent *love* it."

Mom and I stand here, taking it all in.

I'd have to say that my favorite thing so far had been watching the sunset from Piazzale Michelangelo in Florence. You can see the whole city from up there.

But this place instantly takes over the number one spot.

"So, what are the chances we'll actually stay for the year?" It's the same question I've asked every day since we got here. The more I see of Italy, the more I don't want to leave it.

"Same as yesterday, honey," says Mom. "We'll know more once I start working."

It won't be all fun and gelato, though, since she insists I be productive and "learn a little something" while we're here.

I'm distracted from the conversation when a beautiful gondola appears from under the bridge.

"For the record," I say, "I really think it would be in our best interest to stay."

Mom laughs. When her phone goes off with a text notification and she doesn't grab for it, I wonder if she's actually stopping to enjoy the moment.

"Also for the record," she says, "I think it would be in our best interest to find a café that sells pastries."

And I thought this day couldn't possibly get any better.

I grab Mom's hand and pull her across the bridge.

TWO

After having dessert for lunch (yup, that's a thing), Mom and I took the train back to the mainland. Now we're walking down the street to her new office. We pass green-and-white-striped awnings over cafés, and I attempt to read some of the signs along the way, without much luck. There are so many people out on the street—walking, riding bikes, or eating what must be something delicious. Everything is delicious here. People are dressed nice too—I'm tempted to ask the woman in front of me where she got her cute wedge shoes and adorable striped dress.

I stop at a little shop and turn the postcard rack until I find one I know my dad will love.

"Can we get a couple to send home?" I ask.

"Sure," says Mom. "Have you ever sent a post-card before?"

I shake my head.

"Well then, this is the perfect time to start." Mom pays for the postcards and explains how to put the person's name and address on the right side and leave room for the international stamp.

When we get to the office, I consider asking if I can stay outside. There's so much to take in, and I haven't had my fill for the day. The office build-ing looks more like a painting than a place where people work: mustard-colored on the outside with fancy white wooden window frames. In big script, the company name, DiBattisto, is prominently displayed. That's why we're here, for Mom's job, so I smile and step toward the door.

When we walk inside, it's all kinds of mod-ern. Employees and cubicles are everywhere, and apparently some people get their own offices.

We meet Franco, aka someone super impor-tant (I can tell by the way everyone looks nervous when we walk by), and he takes us to where Mom will be set up for the summer. Turns out Mom is getting her own office too.

I probably should learn what she does at some point, but for now it's easy to say "she works in marketing." I'm pretty sure that means she helps companies figure out how to sell whatever it is they make by convincing people they really, really need it. She says it's all about the words you choose.

"Your mother tells me you'd like to take part in our informal internship program," says Franco.

I give Mom a look. It's more like I don't have a choice. It's a company benefit that employees' kids get to do a summer mentorship. Which means Mom doesn't have to find someone to keep an eye on me during the day. And I know not to be ungrateful. "Yes," I say. "I'd love to."

"Is there anything in particular you like to do? Do you have a favorite subject in school?" asks Franco.

Hmm. Does lunch count? I think to myself.

There are big photos of Italian food all over the walls with the DiBattisto logo plastered on top. Pasta. Sauce. Desserts. Maybe there's a taste-testing internship?

I must be quiet too long because Mom jumps in. "Skyler has tried out a lot of things," she says, "but hasn't quite found what she loves just yet."

Good answer, Mom. She really is good at choosing the right words.

It's all true. In my entire thirteen years I haven't found what I'm good at. I've seriously done everything from gymnastics to acting classes, even taking a couple bagpipe lessons and doing a pottery camp one summer. And school, well, I do my best. Sort of. But here I am, standing in the middle of a fancy office building in Italy with all kinds of opportunities in front of me, and I can't even answer a simple question about what I like to do.

"I love trying new things," I say. Mom gives me a smile, and I wonder if maybe some of that marketing know-how has rubbed off on me.

"Great," says Franco. He gives us a tour of the building, and I can tell Mom is excited to be here from the skip in her step and her nonstop grin. It's not all that different from where she works at home—people have their kids' drawings tacked up at their workstations and everyone is busy doing something. But I'm also reminded we are definitely far from home. The conversations all around us are in rapid-fire Italian, and someone must have just ordered lunch because the smell of fresh pasta and sauce drifts through the air.

When we get back to where we started, Franco stops. "I think we can place you with the accounting department," he says to me. "What do you think?"

Oh boy. What I think is that he could have offered me pool slime cleanup and I'd be better at that. But I keep quiet in case that actually is an option.

Mom gives me a little nudge with her elbow.

"Yeah, well, I, um . . ." I am rarely at a loss for words, but it's suddenly hitting me like a ninety-mile-per-hour fastball (I kept score for the baseball team one season too) that I literally have no solid interests other than finding *new* interests.

I'm distracted by someone heading toward me with a stack of boxes in front of his face, and he is definitely not watching where he's going. As he walks by, my shoulder hits one of the file boxes, which causes a chain reaction ending in everything toppling over.

BOOM.

The next thing I know, I'm on the floor, along with a mess of papers.

Well, now I'm not at a loss for words. "You know, you might want to try *not* stacking things so high that you can't see in front of you."

Franco reaches out his hand to help me up and makes sure I'm okay as the boy starts putting everything he dropped back together.

He finally stands up and speaks.

"Sorry 'bout that, mate," he says with a strong Australian accent, pushing his loose blond hair out of his face. He looks about my age.

I don't say a word, but he must be used to the surprised reaction.

"No Australian jokes, okay? I don't actually say 'put another shrimp on the barbie.'"

Mom and I can't help but laugh.

"Logan is one of our interns," says Franco. "His parents work in our design division, and they're here for the year."

"Are you joining the social media internship too?" he asks me.

"Oh, is that an option?" I ask Franco. Social media I can do.

Franco checks something on his phone. "Looks like there's one spot left," he says. "Of course, there would be quite a bit of writing involved, and you'd be exploring Venice for your posts. Does that sound like a good fit?"

Exploring Venice? Yes, please. I mean, I wouldn't

say I'm *good* at writing, but I kind of like when we do creative writing in class. How cool would it be to write about this place?

"It does sound like a good fit," I say.

Well, it's not like I wouldn't have chosen it *before* the cute Australian boy said he was doing it.

Mom pushes her lips together and gives me a sideways glance. She might not approve of my decision-making process, but she doesn't say a word.

"Let's get you set up," says Franco, clapping his hands and making a surprisingly loud thunderish sound.

"See you later, Mom." I give her a wave that says *Maybe this won't be so bad* as Franco leads me and Logan down the hall to the next phase of my summer.

THREE

Dear Dad,

I have to admit, we have a pretty nice
setup here.

Mom's company rented her an
apartment with comfy furniture, a full
kitchen, and a view of the river. I even
get my own room!

And it's a short bus ride to Venice!

Miss you.
xoxo Skyler

I finish writing my first-ever postcard. I'll talk to Dad on the phone later, so he'll know everything I ~~wrote long before he actually gets the postcard,~~ but when I imagine him going to the mailbox and finding something from me, it makes me smile. I miss him a lot already.

I spend the next twenty-nine minutes and fourteen seconds trying to work on my assignment for the internship. It's possible I'm watching the clock more than working on the assignment.

"How's it going, honey?" asks Mom, poking her head through the doorway.

I'm lying on my stomach with a blank journal in front of me and a pen in my hair. "Not so good," I answer. "Did you know they're going to pick two of us to do an internship during the school year? I mean, it only applies to me if we stay, but still."

"Well, that sounds like a great opportunity," says Mom. "If we do stay in Italy, that would be amazing to put on your future résumé."

I lay my head on my hands and stare at the wall. "Yeah, I guess, but you haven't heard the best part."

Mom sits down next to me on the bed. "What's that?"

I set the journal aside and sit up, pulling the pen out from behind my ear so I have something to fiddle with. "They also own *Travel Adventures* magazine. Did you know that?"

"I did," says Mom. "But what does that have to do with an internship in their food division?"

"Franco said the *Travel Adventures* blog draws in readers who are interested in Italy, and then they can advertise their food products on the page. So we'll be providing the content for a new feature for younger readers. I guess it's sort of a test. If we do well, we'd also have a shot at being a teen reporter for the magazine," I say. "Mom, they'd send us all over Europe on assignments. Can you even imagine?"

Mom smiles. "That's wonderful, Skyler. Although I'd miss you if you were traveling all over Europe without me. I'm assuming it's supervised?"

Although I'd miss you.

I let the words sit there for a minute and almost don't catch the rest of what she said.

"Yeah, of course," I say. "I think . . ." I hesitate to finish the sentence because I'm not sure I want to see her reaction. "I think parents can go if they want."

What I'm hoping she'll say is, *Well, I wouldn't miss a chance to spend time with you!* What I'm actually expecting is, *You know I have to work, Skyler.* I get something in the middle.

"That would be a lot of fun," she says. "But of course it would depend."

She doesn't need to elaborate; I know what it depends on.

If we end up staying in Italy, Dad will come over and I'll have him to keep me company, but Mom? Probably not so much. If I want to have some adventures while we're here, I'm the one who needs to make them happen.

"Oh, I'm not done," I say, leaning forward and looking right at her, trying to show her how much I want this. "It's possible we'd even be covering celebrity events!"

Mom laughs. "I don't understand what the problem is, then."

I let out an enormous sigh, and I know I'm being a little overdramatic. "We're supposed to come up with a list of blog post ideas, and I can't decide what to put on it."

"Why don't you start by telling me about your assignment? Maybe I can help," says Mom.

"Our job is to write about Italy from an outsider's perspective," I explain. "We have to come up with ideas for about three posts per week."

"Can they be about anything?" asks Mom.

"Sort of. Marissa is in charge of the interns, and she gave us three themes we're supposed to cover." I point to my handwritten notes.

Only in Venice

Try Something New

The Heart of Venice

"And whatever we decide on, the company will get us where we need to go to write about it," I say. "Which is just about the coolest thing I could ever imagine, except that I can't think of anything."

Mom gently takes the pen from my hand and flips to a blank page in the journal. "Well, Marissa's instructions give you a lot of creative freedom while still providing some guidelines. Have you done any research? There are only a million things in Venice you could do, Skyler."

I nod and grab my laptop from the desk. "That's

the problem. There are *too* many things to choose from."

Mom writes *IDEAS* at the top of the page in capital letters. She looks up, across the room, at nothing. "A list," she says to herself.

I wait. She's clearly in thinking mode.

"Who do we know who is excellent at making lists? Hmm." It's not an actual question as much as one she obviously already knows the answer to. But I'm not following.

I wait again.

"Oh, come on, Skyler. Who is absolutely the best list-maker you've ever known?" she asks. "You can't possibly have forgotten her already."

A smile grows across my face, and I perk up. "Ella. If there were a contest for the best list-maker in the entire world, Ella would win," I say, picturing her with a golden trophy. "Or she'd at least come in a close second."

"You two patched things up before you left, right?" asks Mom.

Mom hasn't asked much about it, and I guess I've been letting it all sink in, not totally sure what Ella and I are anymore. We've been friends since kindergarten, but this summer we had the biggest fight we'd ever, ever had before. We managed to make up and we both agreed that it's totally okay to do different things, even though I'm still getting used to the idea. Then we went on our separate adventures. We haven't talked since I left for Italy. Which, to be honest, wasn't all that long ago.

"I don't know, Mom. It's still kind of weird between us," I say.

Mom sets the journal down in front of me and taps my phone. "Remember, you've got that app on there that lets you do international calls, texts, and video chats. Just in case you want to use it."

The problem is that the person on the other end has to have the app too, and Ella and I didn't work out any kind of communication plan. But I don't mention that to Mom. I just smile and let her leave the room thinking she did a good thing.

I stare at my computer screen, then the journal, then the phone. If anyone can help me make this list, it's definitely Ella.

Computer screen.

Journal.

Phone.

Deep breath.

I grab my phone and send Ella an e-mail with the information she'd need to contact me. Then I stare at the journal again, because there's still a good chance I'll have to figure this out on my own.

FOUR

Mom and I walk to the office the next morning, after rushing through my morning routine. Turns out you can't blame jet lag forever.

"We're only twelve minutes late," I whisper to Mom as we walk up to her office building. I've already gotten the speech from her about being punctual and professional, so I'm not surprised by the look I get in return.

Marissa is tall and skinny, with dark hair flowing over her shoulders. Her long, colorful earrings catch my attention. She must be about my mom's age.

She tells us a little more about herself while

we wait for the other intern who's supposed to be joining us. "I'm originally from Italy, but I lived in the US for most of my life," she says. "I came back here ten years ago with my parents and simply could not bring myself to leave."

That explains why her accent isn't like the others. There's a hint of both countries when she speaks.

I'm about to ask Marissa a question when a girl with shoulder-length, shiny, dark brown hair, with the most gorgeous curls I've ever seen, comes running down the street yelling, *"Sono qui!"*

I turn to Marissa for a translation. "She's saying she's here."

Oh. Well, obviously.

"Ciao," says Marissa. She says some more in Italian, and all I catch is our names. Then she motions toward the three of us. "Zara, meet Logan, Skyler, and Skyler's mother, Mrs. Grace." I continue to be amazed that so many people here speak two languages and switch back and forth so easily.

Zara gives a small smile, if you can call it that. Maybe it's more of a smirk.

"We should get a move on," says Marissa. "Don't worry. I'll take good care of them. It's time for our first adventure!" She puts one hand on my back and one on Zara's, guiding us toward the bus stop.

It only takes ten minutes to get to Venice, and once we're off the bus, Marissa explains the agenda for the day. "Since you have until tomorrow to do your research and choose your blog post topics, I thought we should just explore and let you experience Venice." She waves an arm through the air.

I guess I'd always pictured Venice as all water and boats, but that's only part of it. Even though I was here yesterday with my mom, I'm speechless (again, that's new for me) as we walk through wide streets, narrow streets, and along waterways. There are people everywhere, but no cars, which makes it both noisy and quiet in a totally new way.

Everything is seriously incredible. The ground, the buildings, the little cafés along the way. It's not like anything I've seen before in real life. Like, ever. I love all the red and green awnings, the faded colors of the walls, and the barber-shop-striped posts in the water.

It even smells different. Not bad different (well, maybe a little), but if I close my eyes, it's like a seaside town with a little breeze blowing by here and there. Which, by the way, is super helpful because it's pretty hot and really, really crowded.

When Marissa and Zara get a bit ahead of us, Logan leans over and whispers, "What do you think of the new girl?"

I smile, mostly because I can't seem to help it around him. "I don't know if she counts as the 'new' girl when we've only been here since yesterday."

He laughs. "Yeah, but still. I like to think you and I have been holding down the fort. Besides, I've been here for *two* days."

I get back to his original question, although I'm not sure if we're already past it. "She hasn't said a word to me. I don't even know if she speaks English."

"You've hardly said a word either," he reminds me. "But I get it. This place is breathtaking."

Only with a charming accent can a kid get away with using the word "breathtaking" and not sound all adult.

"It really is," I say.

Logan's gaze settles on a couple walking in our direction. "My mum likes to play this game where you guess what a stranger's story is." He nods his head toward the couple. "Take this guy. What do you think he does for a crust?"

I turn to Logan, trying to process his words. When his face stays all serious, I have to laugh. "I'm sorry, but I didn't understand a thing you just said."

Logan smiles. "Ah, no worries. There I go speaking Australian English to an American. We've taken the language and put our own twist on it."

"I see that. Tell me more?" I ask, now super curious.

"Well, for example, you'd say the front of the car has a hood and the back is the trunk." His perfectly accented words draw me in. "We'd call them a bonnet and a boot."

"A *booot*." I try to mimic the sound.

"Not bad," says Logan.

I'm pretty sure I could stand here and give him words to say all day long and still be entertained.

"We're going to stop here so you can take some notes," says Marissa, ending my Aussie lesson.

I hadn't even noticed we'd walked onto another bridge. They're everywhere here. No wonder it's called the City of Bridges.

I take out my notebook and study what's around me. The small stone bridge we're standing on and the decorative metal railings. The thin canal below us, now full of gondolas and tourists probably

paying way too much for a ride. The balconies, full
of greens and flowerpots. I jot it all down and get
out my phone to take pictures.

Marissa walks over and stands next to me.
"People who come here for the first time do one
of two things," she says. "They either take so many
pictures that they don't take it all in and enjoy it,
or they're so busy taking it all in that they forget
to take pictures."

I laugh, clearly being in the second category
until this point.

"It's incredible," I say. "All of it."

Marissa pats my journal. "Then you'll have
plenty to write about."

As soon as she walks away, I check my international call app for any sign of contact from Ella.
Nothing.

But at least I can get the list started.

*Blog post #1: Don't forget to forget
your camera for a moment.*

It's been twenty-four hours, and there's still no
reply from Ella. When I think how we used to
answer each other instantly, it makes me a little

sad. Looks like I'm on my own for making this list.

I open the desk drawer in my bedroom and pull out the guidebook Marissa gave each of us earlier so I can look through the major tourist attractions. There's an art festival called Venice Biennale that's going on until November. Sounds interesting enough. I add it to the list under the "Only in Venice" theme. The Grand Canal. Well, yeah. Doge's Palace. Anything with the word "palace" in it has to be on the list. People love that stuff.

With today's walk through Venice, that makes four post ideas.

I list a few more attractions without even reading what they are.

St. Mark's Square
St. Mark's Basilica
Teatro La Fenice

Almost done. I figure all of them can fit in any of the three themes Marissa gave us.

I decide to take a break from brainstorming and work on my first blog post, so I open up a new document on my computer. I feel like Madonna or Beyoncé going with a one-word name as my byline, but the company has insisted on it for privacy purposes.

Forget It

By Skyler

Don't forget to forget your camera for a
moment. No seriously, I mean it.

That's it. That's all I've got.

Maybe I'm not a writer after all. The words are
all jumbled in my head to begin with, and getting
them to make sense and sound good on paper is
not an easy task for me. I go back to the list. I need
three more post ideas.

But instead of coming up with something
else, I flop back on my bed and stare at the ceiling. Maybe I should have picked the accounting
internship.

A new sound rings like a church bell from my
phone. I pick it up to investigate.

You have one new message.

I smile because I'm so excited to see a message
from Ella.

Hey. How's Italy?

I type back immediately.

Great!

I start to text *I desperately need your help,* but

I stop myself. Are we still the kind of friends that ask each other for help?

I can tell she's typing too from the little dots in the speech bubble, but then they disappear. No message.

Forget it. I'm asking anyway.

I could use your help. Have time?

I'm six hours ahead of her in Venice, so it's still the middle of the day back home. She responds quickly, which makes me happy.

Only have a few minutes, sorry. What do you need?

She's going to LOVE this. I hope.

I have to make a list.

Ooh, is her response. **Video chat?**

Ella is all about efficiency, so I'm not surprised she'd rather chat than text back and forth.

"Hey, you cut your hair," I say when she pops onto my screen.

"Yeah, I thought I'd try a new look for high school," says Ella. "I mean, I pretty much panicked the entire morning before the appointment, but I did it."

Sure, cutting your hair is a big deal for anyone, but for Ella, a change like that is a huge deal.

"Well, it looks great," I say. "I'm proud of you."

It's a little weird to see her face all the way over here and to know she's off doing her own things without me, and me without her.

"Thanks," she says. "So, what do you need help with?"

I'm not really sure where to start, but Ella always knows what to do.

I go through Marissa's themes for the blog posts and read Ella my list. She smiles a polite smile.

"What?" I ask. "These are the big things to see here."

"I'm sure they are," says Ella. "And don't get me wrong, Skyler, that would totally be *my* list. But it shouldn't be yours."

She's so right. As much as I think I *should* want to see all these places, I'm not all that excited about it.

"I'm so stuck, Ella," I say, propping up my phone on a pillow and setting my journal on my lap. "We walked around Venice all day today, and I wrote two sentences. *Two* sentences."

Ella takes a deep breath and looks around her room. She's thinking, so I wait.

"What did you love most about today?" she asks.

Now I'm thinking.

"I guess learning new things," I say. "The cool stuff, like how Venice is really a group of islands connected by bridges."

"Okay, great," says Ella. "So your list should have some things you want to learn about Venice. That can be for the 'Only in Venice' theme."

I make a note in my journal.

"What else?" she asks.

"I liked listening to people talk," I say. "I love the accent, and even though all I've taken is a year of Spanish, I actually caught some Italian words that were similar."

"Perfect," says Ella. "So you want to learn some Italian?"

"That would be awesome," I say, adding it to the list under "Try Something New."

"Tell me one of your favorite parts of the day," says Ella.

I laugh. "Well, there was this one guy who kept trying to sell us stuff, and whenever this other intern, Logan, would talk to him, the guy could not get what he was saying because of Logan's Australian accent. It was like one of those really messed-up text messages when autocorrect takes over and no one understands what's going on. The rest of us couldn't stop laughing."

Ella laughs too. "See, now *there's* a blog post," she says. "People, Skyler. You're clearly meant to write about people and stories, not famous churches that everyone else writes about."

Oh boy, she's good.

"Okay, hold on." I write furiously in my notebook under "Heart of Venice." "If I do three posts on each of those topics, I'm all set. Thank you!" I want to lean forward and hug the phone, hoping she'll feel it across the miles, but I don't know if she wants a phone hug. "The Italy list is good to go," I say instead.

"Skyler, I would totally love to hear about this Australian boy," she says with a playful smirk on her face, "but I really have to go."

Ella's mom pops into the background before I can say another word. "Oh, hi, Skyler. I hope you're having a wonderful time in Italy, but Ella has to get to her summer reading report now."

And while *I* would have made a face that says *Ugh, no, not a report*, Ella is beaming and obviously excited to write the thing.

"Sorry, Skyler," she says. "But I'm glad you have friends over there to help you. Good luck."

I shouldn't have to analyze what she means, but I do. Does "good luck" mean *Let me know how it goes*? Or does it mean *Since I won't be calling again, good luck with everything*? The problem is, Ella's the one I'd ask to help me figure out what she means.

"Thanks," I say. My brain does it again. Do I say *Talk to you soon* or *Call me*? Or do I just say goodbye and go on my way?

Ella breaks the awkward silence for both of us. "Say hi to your mom for me."

"I will."

We wave at our screens, and I wait for Ella to hit her button to disconnect the call. As soon as the phone goes back to my home screen, I'm the one who feels disconnected.

For a few minutes it felt like the old, names-smooshed-together SkylerandElla. I haven't quite figured out this new Skyler and Ella yet.

But I have a job to do and things to write about, whether I can get the words out or not. I transfer my notes to my computer and e-mail it off to Marissa, who writes back immediately.

This is fantastic, Skyler. I'll get you set up with Italian lessons right away. And, oh boy, are there some interesting things to learn about Venice. Do you know what the city was built on? ☺

I write back, *No, but I plan to find out.* ☺

FIVE

So it turns out I'm kind of living in the world's coolest tree house.

Venice was literally built in a lagoon, on millions of tree trunks. A quick search last night brought up all kinds of links, plus some great YouTube videos that explain the whole history. That's the kind of stuff they should teach in social studies.

I've been waiting to tell Marissa I found the answer to her question, but we had a tour of the library this morning and now she's working quietly and I don't want to interrupt her.

Marissa has designated today a writing day, so we're inside the most amazing study room I have ever, ever seen. I practice whispering "Querini Stampalia Library" to myself, but my Italian needs a lot of practice.

As if the outsides of the buildings here aren't majestic enough (and yes, I used the word "majestic" because that's totally what they are), the insides are even more amazing. The ceilings and walls are literal works of art, the books here are so old and important that you have to be at least sixteen to even touch them, and the work area we're in feels more like the inside of a castle than a library.

I'm not even sure how Marissa got us permission to work here since we're not technically old enough to be trusted around old books, but I'm certainly not complaining. Although I am a bit distracted by the big chandeliers above the tables and the round, detailed painting on the center of the ceiling. The four of us sit at a thick, oval, wooden table, Marissa on one side and the interns on the other. Everyone else is busy writing, and they've even learned the right way to type. The one where you keep your fingers on the keyboard instead of poking at the keys like I have to. I'm a little afraid to let them know I can't type properly, but then I remind myself that most thirteen-year-olds probably can't either. Or can they?

I've stalled long enough, researching for blog post number two, because I really need to get post number one written. Except I can't seem to stop my brain when it gets wondering. I still don't know if Zara speaks English since she hasn't said anything in my presence yet. I'm super curious, so to catch a glimpse of what language she's writing in, I lean a little to my left.

A little too far to my left.

"Whoa, whoa, oh boy." I grab on to the table, and Zara's leg, to steady myself and somehow manage not to fall into her lap. But when you're the only one talking in a big, silent room, people stare. And give you the evil eye. Oops.

Sorry, I mouth.

Everyone gets back to work, even Zara, but I didn't catch a single word on her screen. So I watch her typing. Maybe I can figure it out that way.

A-C-Y. No wait, D-O-G . . .

"*Che cosa?*" whispers Zara.

Darn. Caught red-handed.

"Ooh, that sounds like *que* in Spanish," I say. "What?"

"*Sì, che?*" she responds.

I smile because maybe I can actually figure out this Italian thing. "You said, 'Yes, what?'"

"*Lo so.*"

"Hmm, I don't know that one."

Marissa gives me a look as Zara gets up and motions for me to follow her out through the doorway.

"Why are you watching me type?" she asks.

Ah, clearly English. What happened to her Italian accent? But now I have to explain myself.

"I didn't know if you only spoke Italian," I say. "Sorry, it's kind of fun actually, getting to use what I learned in school. Sort of. I mean, I took Spanish, not Italian, but they're similar, don't you think?"

Zara stares at me.

"I'm going to take Italian lessons, because obviously this is Italy and—"I stop myself. I'm not usually a rambler, but for some reason this girl makes me nervous.

"I speak Italian and English. As well as a few other languages," she says. "Anything else?"

What I really want to ask is how she'd say that in Italian, but I don't push it. "No, that's it, thanks."

Zara puts her hand on her hip and turns toward me. *"No se habla en la biblioteca."*

When I stare at her for what is clearly too long, she seems to get that I'm going to need it in English.

"No talking in the library," she says. "I said it in Spanish for you. Seems you're a bit rusty."

I nod. I guess I am. "Got it. Yes, no talking in the library. That's our rule too."

We sit back down at the table, and I get all set up in front of my laptop when Logan slides a note in front of me that says *You got in trouble* with a winky face. I laugh, just a little, but am quick to cover my mouth and not have a repeat of everyone staring at me.

I flip over the piece of paper and draw a shrimp on a barbecue, because I'm pretty sure that's what "shrimp on a barbie" means. I add my own winky face.

This time Logan laughs, out loud, and everyone stares at him instead.

I have to say, I'm loving Italy (and if I'm being honest, Australia) so far. Now, if only I could figure out how to write these posts.

I hold the shift key and poke at the letter keys, not even caring who's watching.

Forget It
By Skyler

Don't forget to forget your camera for a moment. No seriously, I mean it.

From the moment I stepped foot in Italy, I was amazed. Everything is old and beautiful, and you stare at it wondering how on earth anyone could have possibly built it.

And then there's the countryside. Oh boy, there was no preparing me for how gorgeous and knock-your-socks-off incredible it is to look out a train window and see the Italian countryside.

Now here we are in Venice, and it's like I've been transported into the pictures in our social studies books—the ones I never really paid any attention to unless forced. But Venice is interesting and full of beauty and amazing, and sometimes you need to set down your camera, stop, and take it all in.

Because sometimes the best pictures are the pictures in your mind that you will never, ever forget.

* * *

It's Friday afternoon, and I'm sitting across from Marissa at a café near the office.

"I wanted to speak to each of you separately so we could really dive into what you need to work on, as well as what your strengths are," she says to me.

I imagine the weaknesses list is probably a lot longer, but maybe there'll be a couple of things on the strengths side too?

"What I love about your first piece is that your enthusiasm and sense of wonder really come through," says Marissa. "That's not easy to accomplish."

She is totally going to Sandwich Method me. It's exactly what my English teacher always told us to do when we read each other's papers:

> Something positive.
> What needs to be worked on.
> Something else you liked.

Not only does it work like the layers of a sandwich, the directions even look like one. So I'm not the least bit surprised at what comes next.

"I do think there are some things we need to work on," says Marissa.

"By 'we,' I'm guessing you mean me?" I ask.

"No, I mean we," she answers. "This is an internship, Skyler. No one expects you to be perfect from the get-go. It's my job to help you improve your writing."

Marissa takes a sip of her cappuccino, and I take another bite of my spaghetti. Yum.

"For starters, it's a little shorter than what we're looking for," she says. "It's one hundred fifty words; however, we'd like you to aim for at least three hundred."

It's not like I didn't know the target number, I just couldn't get there. "Okay, I think I can do that," I say.

"Great. I'd also like to see a little more detail, and I want you to keep an eye out for repetitive words," she says.

I choose my words carefully because I don't want it to come out like I'm not willing to take her advice. "It's really hard to come up with enough adjectives to describe this place," I say.

"It is," answers Marissa. "That's why I want you to learn to describe it in different ways. For example, if you say that a building was established in 1570, you don't have to say that it's old.

Or if you describe the way the light hits the green of the trees, you don't have to say how gorgeous it is. Does that make sense?"

I don't answer right away because I want to get all of this in my journal. "It totally does," I say. When I'm done jotting down Marissa's feedback, I give her my complete attention. "I'm clearly not the best at this, but I swear I'm going to work hard."

"I know you will," she says.

"What's the rest of the sandwich?" I ask. Because I wouldn't mind hearing something else she liked about my very short, repetitive post.

Marissa looks at our bowls of pasta. "Sandwich?" she asks.

"Oh, sorry, the compliment sandwich," I say. "You're supposed to give me a nice comment at the end, right?"

Marissa laughs. "You know more than you think you do about writing, Skyler," she says. "Yes, I have two more things I wanted to share with you. One, I love when your voice comes through. I think once you're more comfortable with it, we'll see that a whole lot more. And two, you have a way of saying things that will really connect with readers.

Comparing your observations to being transported to the pictures in your social studies books or creating a picture in your mind—those are perfect ways to describe an experience. Well done."

I smile, because I didn't even know those were strengths of mine.

"Each one of you has a great shot at getting that school-year internship," says Marissa. "And from what I've heard about your mom, I'd say there's a good chance you'll be here for the year. Which is why I'm considering you officially in the running for the internship."

I'm not the least bit surprised that Mom has already made a good impression.

"That would be great," I say. "And I would love to be a teen reporter for the travel magazine." My mind whirls with where I would get to go with a job like that. My own job—to keep *me* busy.

"Yes, that, too," she says. "But you're going to have to give it your all to earn it."

I acknowledge the challenge with a nod. I'm determined to prove I can do this.

"For now I'd suggest you put some of those photos you took on social media," she says. "I'll e-mail you the log-in info for the account."

At least that part will be easy.

"Well, that's enough shop talk for now," says Marissa. "Let's finish up lunch, and then I can show you one of the absolute best things about Italy."

When it's time, I follow her without question, because if there's even the slightest chance that it's dessert instead of a church or a really old statue, I am so totally in.

SIX

Dear Ella,

Guess what I'm eating?! And it's delicious!
   Marissa and I just met to talk about
my first blog post (she's in charge of the
interns), and then she said she'd show me
one of the best things about Italy. I was
hoping I knew what it was, and you know
what? My wish was totally granted—gelato!
Of course I've already had it a few times
since I've been here, but you cannot—I
repeat, cannot—have too much gelato.
   And since the last flavor on our try-every-
ice-cream-flavor-on-the-list challenge back

home was pistachio, I couldn't resist getting it
and snapping a picture for you!

It's actually really good. Seriously, you make
it gelato and the flavor doesn't even matter.
Yum.

I start an e-mail to Ella on my phone and attach the
photo. As much as I'm loving Italy, I do miss home.
And even though Ella and I have ventured off in
different directions, I miss her, too. I hate worrying
whether or not she'll respond, but I can't eat pistachio gelato and not tell her about it. I just can't.

Marissa is on a phone call, chatting where it
isn't so noisy. I try to listen to the conversations
around me, but I can only understand a word or
two. I clean up our table and make my way over to
a shaded place to sit and wait for Marissa.

When she's done with her call, she has a big
smile on her face.

"Good news," she says. "I found you an Italian
tutor."

"Great," I say. "I can't wait to get started." And
it's true. Going to Spanish class at school—not so
fun. Learning Italian in Italy—yes, please!

We walk back to the office, where Marissa says

we'll meet up with my tutor for my first lesson. I take in my surroundings and can't believe how lucky I am to be here.

That is, until I see Zara standing in front of the building. I brace myself for her snark.

"*Ciao*," says Zara in a surprisingly peppy tone.

"*Ciao*," I repeat, at least knowing it means "hello." Or "good-bye." Maybe both?

"Skyler, meet your Italian tutor." Marissa motions toward Zara, and all I can think is that she's got to be kidding. I take a quick look around to see if there's someone else standing nearby.

Nope.

"I was hoping my son would be willing to help, but he assures me he has a full schedule right now," says Marissa. "This could be even better, though, because you two can spend some more time together."

"I can tell by the look on your face that you're thrilled," says Zara.

But I play it cool so that Marissa will see me as a team player. "I'm really excited to get started," I say, turning to Marissa. "Thanks so much for setting this up."

Marissa smiles. "Stay close and have fun." She's

through the main doors in no time at all.

Zara and I stand here, silent. I purse my lips, trying to think of what to say next. Do I ask her why on earth she'd even want to tutor me? Do I thank her and give her the benefit of the doubt? Or do I run away screaming while I still have the chance to get out of this?

"Listen," she finally says. "I know we didn't get off to a good start, but Marissa asked me to do this and I wasn't about to say no."

"So you're willing to teach me Italian?" With this girl, I feel like I need to make sure.

"Yes," she says. "If it gives me a better shot at that social media internship for the school year, we're doing this."

"And the teen reporter job for the magazine?" I ask, sizing up my competition.

"Nah. The last thing I need is to go somewhere else. If Marissa picks me for that internship, my parents might actually let me stay in one place." She looks at me like it's my turn to speak. "Anyway . . ."

I'm tempted to ask what she's talking about, but for now I get the sense that she's told me all she's willing to share.

"Thanks for helping me," I say.

"Should we get started?"

Just like that I'm about to learn a new language and maybe, if pigs really do fly, make a new friend.

Zara and I find a spot to sit in the piazza near the office. Or, really, Zara picks a spot.

"Do you know any other languages?" asks Zara. "Some Spanish, right?"

"Yeah. I took a year of it," I answer. "So I guess a little."

She jots that down in her notebook like I've just answered some super-important question.

"Okay, I can work with that. The Romance languages have a lot of similarities," she says. "That's Spanish, Italian—"

I take my chance to look like I at least know something. "And French."

"That's good," she says. "But there are actually more of them. Portuguese and Romanian, for example."

I'm here to learn, so I figure I'll be a good student and ask questions. "Why are they called that?"

Zara perks up. She clearly likes being the teacher. "Well, they're all descended from Latin, which was the language spoken by the Romans.

As the Roman Empire spread, so did the language. Over time different languages evolved, and they're called the Romance languages."

"So they all come from the same source essentially?" I ask, biting my lip. It isn't *Jeopardy!*, but the stakes feel just as high with this girl.

"Right. So the grammar and vocabulary are often very similar." She says all of this in perfect English, but the Italian being spoken around us reminds me I'm a world away from home. "If you know some Spanish," she continues, "that's a great start."

I sit here thinking that I might actually be able to do this. Is it possible that maybe I pegged this girl wrong?

"I'm going to teach you a couple basic phrases," says Zara. "Then we can go practice them."

Now this is getting fun. "Okay, I'm ready," I say.

"First, try *delizioso*." She writes the word down on a page in her notebook and turns it toward me.

I try my best to mimic the way she said it. "*Delizioso*. It means 'delicious,' right?"

She actually looks a little proud of me. "You got it. Try it again."

I practice until I get the pronunciation right,

and now I'm totally ready to go use it. "What's next?" I ask.

She teaches me *più,* pronouncing it like a church "pew." Apparently that's what you say when you don't want more of something. I'm supposed to say it enthusiastically.

She pauses and gives me what starts as a smirk but turns into an odd kind of smile.

"But don't forget to always say 'please' with it," she adds. *"Per favore."*

"Per favore," I repeat. "Can we go test them out?" My heels are bouncing, and I must have a ridiculous grin on my face because my cheeks hurt from smiling.

"If you insist," says Zara. "Let's go."

SEVEN

Zara calls Marissa to let her know we're going to a local café to practice my newly learned Italian. I'm seriously bouncing down the street.

"You're actually going to let me try it out?" I ask.

"You have to speak it to get it, Skyler," says Zara. "Being immersed in a culture is the best way to learn a language. So of course I'll let you try it out."

There's that smirky, odd smile again.

I take the opportunity to try to get more out of her. "How did you learn Italian? And, hey, while we're getting to know each other, where are you from?"

"You're dying to figure me out, aren't you?" says Zara.

I nod but refuse to admit how interesting I find her.

"You're going to regret asking," she says.

"Try me."

I'm not convinced she'll really tell me, but as we take a few more steps down the street, she starts her story. "I was born in Spain. But we moved when I was four," she says. "My dad is Spanish. My mom is from India. I've lived all over the place, including Italy."

"All over the place, like a few countries in Europe?" I ask.

"No, literally all over the world. A year here, a year there. My parents like to try new things," she says. "So I'm not sure I can give you an answer to where I'm from."

She keeps walking and looking straight ahead with her matter-of-fact answers. I can't tell if she's humoring me or if she wants to have a conversation. I take my chances.

"Where do you live now?" I ask.

"I'm staying with my aunt for a bit while my parents are off working."

"Are they spies or something?" I laugh, not meaning it as a serious question.

"I wish," she says. "Then maybe things would make sense." She changes the topic. "My dad says it'll be a huge advantage to be fluent in multiple languages, so he's big on me using them all on a regular basis. He specifically asked Marissa to make sure that I do."

It's silence for the next couple minutes. Maybe she'll open up more if I tell her about myself.

"I'm from New York," I say, since she didn't ask. "But not New York City. Everyone always thinks that's what you mean when you say New York, but there's a whole other state outside of there."

My answer pales in comparison to hers, but I'm happy to have one place to call home.

As if this semibonding moment is too much for us, we both look away from each other as we walk up to the café. Not only do I get to try out my Italian, but I also get more Italian dessert.

"I'm going to order," says Zara. "You just listen."

I nod and stand next to her to make sure I can hear everything they say. Not that I understand any of it, but still, it sounds beautiful.

We take our dessert and manage to snag a table.

The food is amazing—as it always is—and I'm not ashamed to say that it doesn't take me long to have only crumbs left on the plate. Zara, on the other hand, eats much more daintily, taking little bites like she's savoring every piece.

The guy behind the counter looks our way and says something to which Zara nods.

"Here's your chance, Skyler," she says. "He's asking how it is."

"Oh." I straighten up in my chair and look directly at the guy with a huge smile. *"Delizioso,"* I say, to let him know how delicious it is. "Did I say it right?" I ask Zara.

"You did great," she says.

I want to ask more about her, but she seems content to just sit and eat her dessert. I wonder if she has a best friend in one of the places she's lived. Does she like moving around? Where's the most exciting place she's ever been?

"What are you doing over there?" she asks. "You look really deep in thought."

Without thinking, I blurt out, "You scare me a little."

Zara laughs. "In what way?"

"I don't know how to read you," I say. "I mean, don't take this the wrong way, but you haven't been all that nice to me and you don't say much, so I have no idea what you're thinking."

She's quiet for a bit before saying anything. "I don't know how to do the friend thing, Skyler. I move around a lot and people don't seem to like me all that much anyway, so I'm not sure why I'd bother trying."

Now I really don't know what to say. Is she being tough because she doesn't care—or because she's afraid to care?

"I like you," I say. "I just wish I knew more about you."

Both of our plates are now clean, and I figure I'll go get something to take home for my mom and give Zara a minute.

I point to the dessert I want—tiramisu is my mom's favorite. I have no idea how to say "to go," so I point. The guy grabs a to-go box and holds it out in front of him. His eyebrows go up, and I nod. This nonverbal communication thing might just be what gets me through this summer.

He places one piece in the container and sets it on the counter. Since this is going so well, I figure I'll use the one phrase I have left and let him know

I don't want any more. *"Più, per favore!"* I say it with as much enthusiasm as I can.

He reaches into the display case, grabs another piece of tiramisu, and puts it in the box.

Huh?

I turn to Zara, who isn't paying any attention to me.

"No, no," I say. *"Più."* I'm trying to tell the guy I don't want any more, but I must be pronouncing it wrong because he reaches in and grabs another piece again.

This goes on until there are six pieces of tiramisu in my to-go box.

"Zara," I call, finally getting her attention. "How do I tell him I don't want any more?"

She walks over, looks in the box, and giggles. There's that odd little smirk again.

I have no idea what she says to him, but he closes up the box and she pays for the order.

"My treat," she says.

We walk away, and I'm so confused. "Um, thanks, I guess. You didn't have to do that."

Zara lets out a chuckle. "I know. I guess I really shouldn't have."

All I can do is shake my head around this girl.

I'm still not sure what I really said to the guy at the counter, but if Zara just played me for a fool, I am not giving her the satisfaction of seeing she rattled me.

I hope Mom is hungry.

When I get back to the apartment with Mom, she starts dinner (although I would eat out *every* meal here if I could). I hop on the laptop to investigate what Zara actually taught me in Italian.

After her constant smirking and my box full of tiramisu, I'm not the least bit surprised to discover that she purposely taught me the wrong phrase. Well, either it was on purpose or she doesn't really know Italian.

Turns out *più* doesn't mean "no more," it means "more."

I cover my face with my hands, so embarrassed— even though I had no idea what I was doing.

Way to go, Skyler. I really should have been paying more attention to Zara's expressions. She has a tell— like when people try to bluff in poker. Apparently she does that smirk when she's up to something.

"She owes me a major apology," I complain out loud to no one. I salute and say, "Major Apology," wishing Ella were here to get the joke.

My mom pokes her head in my room. "Everything okay in here?" she asks.

"It will be," I answer. "Once I do a little work."

Mom nods. "Great. Dinner will be ready soon. It's a recipe Franco gave me."

Well, if it can't be an Italian restaurant, an Italian recipe is the next best thing. Even if it is Mom cooking.

"And it looks like we're all set for dessert." Mom gives me a wink before she leaves the room.

After what turns out to be a delicious dinner worthy of using *più* several times, I write both a real blog post to turn in to Marissa and a fake one to show Zara.

The one describing the Italian lesson and the scene in the café that followed actually makes me laugh. But I don't give a hint that I'm on to Zara, I just write the post like I've learned some helpful new words that all visitors in Italy should know. The look on Zara's face when she thinks I fell for her prank will be worth the extra thirty minutes it took.

The real post, the one that says to be careful

when learning a new language, isn't half bad. It still describes the scene that took place in the café, but I decide to use it as an example of "do as I say, not as I do." I title it "A Cautionary Tale."

Mom calls from the other room, "Hey, Skyler, how about a nice evening walk through Italy?"

I've been immersed in the posts, almost forgetting that I'm sitting here writing *in* Italy. The idea of it all is still hard to believe. But a walk with my mom? Those don't happen all that often, so there's no way I'm saying no.

"Absolutely," I call back. "I just have to send this post over to Marissa."

As I'm about to attach the file, Mom calls again. "Skyler, enough work for today. You have to come see this."

I don't think I've ever heard my mom utter the phrase "enough work for today" in my entire life.

I quickly add the attachment, send off the e-mail, and run to see what all the fuss is about.

The lights.

The breeze.

The music playing from the piazza.

It is one million percent amazing.

EIGHT

Mom has weekends off. I realize that's a normal thing for a lot of people, but not for my mom. Back home she worked all the time. Nights, weekends, holidays—it really didn't matter. So when she comes into my room Saturday morning and asks what I'd like to do, I shake my head to make sure I'm not dreaming.

Not only do I get to spend the weekend with my mom, I get to spend it with her in Venice? Doing whatever we want?

While the first thing on my list in this amazing place is always food, I'm also excited to learn fun facts about the city. And if I'm being honest, I might even be a little excited to write about it.

"Can we just wander through Venice?" I ask. "There's so much to see. I can't even pick."

"Absolutely," says Mom. "Let me know when you're ready."

It doesn't take me long to take a quick shower and get dressed. One of the great things about being somewhere else is that you don't have to worry about running into someone you know. There was a boy back home Ella and I nicknamed Penny Boy (that's a story for another time), and I definitely spent more time picking out my outfits in case I ran into him. But here, in Italy? I don't have a care in the world.

I come out into the living room and am not surprised to find Mom on her laptop.

"I thought you didn't have to work," I say. I've seen this plenty of times before—Mom says we'll head out whenever I'm ready, but what it really means is whenever she's done with the super-important project she *has* to finish first.

"I'm sorry, honey. I forgot I have to send in this report, and I don't want to have to worry about it this weekend," she says.

I give her a closed-lip smile, plop down on the couch, and pick up a magazine.

It only takes Mom an hour to tear herself away from work, rather than what could have easily been half a day back home, so I consider it a win.

We do the short walk to the bus station and are in Venice before the third song on my iPod is finished.

Mom and I walk without saying a word for at least thirty minutes, taking in everything we see. I stop at the top of one of the little bridges and try to focus on all the incredible things around me. The noise of thousands of tourists talking in what must be dozens of different languages, the sloshing of the water against the stone walls of the buildings, the warm sun on my skin. It'll be much hotter soon, I'm sure.

We walk on to an area where people are handing out flyers for all the things we can do (and pay them for) today. Mom and I grab a bunch and find a spot to sit and leaf through them. I catch her smiling.

"What?" I ask.

Mom has a look of both sadness and contentment. "This," she says. "Being here with you. Not saying a word and yet having one of the best days of my life with my daughter." She puts her hand over mine.

"Me too, Mom."

As we sit here silently, I hope the moment lasts just a little bit longer, but . . .

"BOO!"

I jump off the bench, along with my mom, and turn to face where the voice came from. "Oh my goodness, Logan!" In case there was ever a question, an Australian accent does not make a "boo" any better. "FYI, I am not a fan of being scared. At all."

He laughs. "So sorry, Skyler." He turns to my mom. "Mrs. Grace."

I've dropped all the flyers I was holding and am not about to be the one to pick them up. I raise my eyebrows at Logan and point to the ground. He doesn't even hesitate before picking up each glossy advertisement.

When he gets to the last one, he stops. "Now, this is not your typical tour of Venice."

"Ooh, I'm totally up for nontypical," I say, reaching for the flyer. "What is it?" But once it's in front of me, I hand it back to Logan. "Um, yeah. No."

My mom leans over to see what all the fuss is about and giggles like a little girl.

"What's so funny?" I ask.

Mom turns to Logan. "Skyler doesn't do haunted houses," she says.

"That's not true." I'm suddenly insulted and a little embarrassed. "I went to a haunted house with Ella, and it wasn't so bad."

Mom puts up her hands. "Okay, well, why don't I let you two talk while I get a cappuccino."

"My parents are over there." Logan points at the lady in the purple shorts and the man in the I'M JUST HERE FOR THE PIZZA T-shirt in front of the café across from us.

"Great," says Mom. "I haven't had a chance to meet them yet." Mom gives me a smile before she walks over to the café.

"So I could probably talk my parents into going on this haunted Venice tour with you and your mom," says Logan. "You know, since you're not afraid of ghosts."

Oh, the dilemmas of a thirteen-year-old girl who might have a bit of a crush on this boy.

"Okay, here's the deal. My friend Ella and I had a list of things to complete this summer, and one of them was facing our fears. My fear was spooky places."

"Was?" asks Logan.

"Yes, was," I answer. "But maybe, well, maybe still a little bit is." I wait, not sure if I'll be laughed at or not, but at the same time figuring it's better to be honest.

Logan nods. "All right, so I guess the only question is, how brave are you?"

Oh man, is that a dare? An Australian dare to face Venice ghosts?

I take an extra-deep breath to give myself a minute to think.

Ella is going to be so proud of me.

"I'm the bravest girl you're ever going to meet," I say, with what comes out as complete confidence, even if my insides are doing somersaults and bungee jumps. "Where do we start?"

NINE

I instantly regret agreeing to go on a ghost tour, but I keep telling myself that it'll make a great blog post. I'm already thinking like a writer. That has to be a good sign.

I get out my journal to take notes for what will probably be the creepiest blog post I ever write in my life.

The Part of Venice You Don't Want to See

I'm not one for haunted houses. Haunted anything, really. And even though I thought I'd faced my fear, it *turns out some things are to be feared for a reason. So when a friend suggested we tour the spookiest places in Venice, I of course—as any non-sane person would—agreed.*

But I did stand my ground and insist we don't go anywhere too crazy, like Poveglia Island.

"No way, Logan," I say after reading about Poveglia in one of the brochures. "It says Italians won't set foot on that island. I am most certainly not going to."

"Come on," he says. "They only take us near it, not *on* it. It's not like this stuff is real." But he pauses, because even if you believe something's not real, there's probably a little doubt in your mind that it might be.

"No, no, and triple no," I say. "It says they sent everyone who got the bubonic plague there. And then again when there was another epidemic. And then they built a psychiatric hospital there.

I'm pretty sure the only reason Logan is acting tough is because the brochure specifically states that tourists aren't even allowed on the island without filing a big application. Although I do get the feeling that for the right price, someone would take you over there. NO THANK YOU.

"Okay, how about this place?" Logan points to another spot in the brochure, and instead of answering him, I sit down and take out my journal again.

> *Since I've already agreed to do this, I have to say yes to at least one of the places on the list. I go with Ca' Dario, a house that sits right on the Grand Canal, near one of the museums. According to legend, the house is cursed and anyone who dares to buy it will suffer financial ruin and death. Yikes! Do you think that's in the description of the listing?*

"Skyler," Logan calls as he taps me on the shoulder. Both of his parents and my mom are standing behind him.

"Oh, sorry," I say. "I'm getting a head start on my blog post. I'm in."

In the few minutes that follow, Logan's mom

has managed to charter a boat to take us there (a benefit to being an important person at her job, I guess) and his dad has the Wikipedia page on his phone to read on the ride there.

"We can't go inside," reports Mr. MacGregor. "But according to all of this, I imagine it'll be creepy enough from the outside."

We walk to where we're meeting the boat, and I try desperately to psych myself up for this. I pretend we're just getting in to take a nice ride along the canal. It works for about two minutes until Logan's dad begins reading out loud to us about the place. I decide to put on my reporter hat and treat this as any old assignment. Oh man, "old" is probably the wrong choice of words.

Words like "doomed" and "mysterious" dot the articles written about this place, making even the skeptics wonder. Even the manager of a famous rock band died tragically a few years after buying the place. (For those who are a little older than my generation, the band is called The Who, although that was

exactly my response when I heard the
name of the band.)

The boat weaves through narrow canals, dodging gondolas and water taxis. We get so close to the buildings, I can reach out and touch my fingers to the stone as we continue through the water. The buildings almost seem to loom overhead, as if they know where we're going and are trying to warn us.

By the time we get to the front of Ca' Dario, Mr. MacGregor has read enough stories for all of us to be convinced that this place is cursed. Logan takes a poll to be sure—yup, everyone agrees.

The driver of the boat reiterates that the legend is real and that no self-respecting Venetian would even consider purchasing the property. He does, however, offer to take us closer.

"No!" I shout, getting five sets of wide eyes focused on me. "I can see much more detail from here." I try to recover from my mini freak-out, but my loud, deep breaths say otherwise.

The building stands tall, with its
sole balcony and rounded archways
depicting a creepy Venice legend.

Mom leans in, and I can tell she's reading over my shoulder. "I'm impressed, honey. I don't think I've ever seen you use those kinds of words for your English assignments."

While it's a bit of a backhanded compliment, I'll take it, because she's right. I had no idea I had it in me to write like this. Then again, I had no idea there was so much to write about either.

As the rest of the group talks about other scary stories, I study the architecture and try to come up with more words that will create a picture in the readers' minds. And that's when I see it.

"OMG." I stand up in the boat—not a good idea, FYI—and point as the vessel rocks back and forth.

"Sit. Please!" shouts the driver, motioning to the other passengers to get me to sit down.

I do as I'm asked. I've toppled over in a boat before, and that wasn't half as bad as falling into the Grand Canal in front of a haunted building would be.

"You don't understand," I say. "I saw something." I study the building again, attempting to find the window where there was movement. "Does anyone live in the house now?" I ask the driver.

He shakes his head. "No. Is private," he says.

"Sometime there are art events, but not open to public."

If there was an art event, I'd have seen people walking back and forth through those windows. "Go closer," I say. As he does, the spooked part of my brain screams at me to change my mind. But the writer part—the part I didn't even know existed— pushes past everything else and demands that I see this through.

I'm hyperaware of the surprised look on my mom's face and the obvious glee Logan is feeling right now.

"Everyone look closely," I instruct. "Do you see anything? Or . . . anyone?"

> *It's a strange experience to sit quietly on a boat while the rest of the world is humming around you.*

I tilt my journal so my mom can read it, and when she smiles, I'm beyond proud of myself.

As we finally pull away from the palace, I try to capture what I've just seen:

> *Fortunately—or unfortunately, if you're into ghosting—my "sighting" was most*

likely a shadow, briefly formed as the clouds passed by us. Oh well, at least I have yet another story to tell.

If you're at all like me, you'll need something more cheerful to focus on after reading this. So I'll leave you with one other thing I learned about haunted Venice. In 1908, the famous French painter Claude Monet created a beautiful rendering (Mom gave me this word) of the area, titled Palazzo Dario. *Note: Ask Marissa if photo of painting can be included.

Perhaps after hearing this story you'll want to see more sites like these. Or maybe you'll instantly search for where you can see this famous painting. Or maybe you won't even get to this part because you stopped reading once you saw what I'd be writing about. But here's the thing. We all have different interests, different fears, different things that amaze us. Learning about the world not only helps

us to be knowledgeable and well-rounded,
it also helps us figure out more about
ourselves.

"So, more haunted sites, Skyler?" asks Logan.

"No." I shake my head. "More Italian desserts, my friend. I think we've all earned it."

A minute later Logan gets a notice on his phone and turns the screen to face me. "Hey, your first post is up," he says.

I grab the phone to see for myself. "Wow. Marissa said it was too short, so I didn't think they'd post it."

There it is—my very first piece of published online writing. I smile.

Without any further directions from our crew, the boat continues down the canal, and all I can think is that I can't wait to see what we find next.

TEN

Dear Ella,

You won't believe what I did.

The house on the front of this postcard is, wait for it . . . haunted.

And get this, I was a brave grown-up and went on a tour outside it.

Mom and I spent the rest of the weekend as tourists. I didn't worry about writing, and Mom didn't ever stop to make a work phone call or check her e-mail. Not once.

All true. Seriously.
xoxo Skyler

When Monday morning comes, I'm a little disappointed that the weekend is over. But at the same
time I'm excited to see what Marissa has to say
about my Italian lessons blog post and to work on
revising what I wrote over the weekend. Is it possible I'm actually good at this? I might really have a
shot at that teen reporter gig.

I walk to work with Mom and head straight to
Marissa's office.

"Good morning," I say.

"Good morning, Skyler," says Marissa. "Have
a seat."

No friendly chat like *How was your weekend?*
or *Enjoying Italy?* What's up with that?

I sit, cross my legs, and intertwine my fingers.
"Is something wrong?" I ask.

Marissa takes a sheet of paper out of her drawer
and slowly slides it across the desk like they do in
the movies. "I'm afraid so."

What could possibly be on that paper that's making her normally cheerful face so gloomy right now?

I lean forward and take it.

Uh-oh.

"Marissa, this isn't the one I meant to send you."
The words scatter from my mouth faster than the

hare in the race against the tortoise. "You were supposed to get 'A Cautionary Tale,' but I must have accidentally attached the wrong file."

Marissa leans back in her chair. "Skyler, this post is full of incorrect information."

"I know," I say. "But Zara gave me the wrong information. She made me say the wrong—"

Marissa cuts me off. "Listen, excuses don't work in journalism. You are responsible for fact-checking your own posts."

"I did, but I sent the wrong one." I try to make my case, but her expression doesn't change. "It was a mistake."

Marissa comes around the desk and sits next to me. "This is an internship. Which means you're learning and I'm supposed to be guiding you," she says. "But you are still responsible for the content of your posts and for getting them in on time. The *right* ones in on time."

I stay quiet.

"Why would you even waste your time writing a post with inaccuracies?"

"I was trying to show Zara she didn't fool me," I say. "That one was only meant to be seen by her, to make her think it's what I'd sent you."

Marissa relaxes a little and even lets out a chuckle. "Well, it is the one you sent me, and now I can't post today's assignment from you."

"I can send you the other one," I say, tapping my laptop. "It's right here."

Marissa gets up again, going back behind her desk. "I'm sorry, Skyler. We're all set, and I've already given away your slot. I'll speak to Zara, but I suggest you work things out with her first and get some real Italian lessons for your next post."

I lower my shoulders and let my chin drop to my chest. The last thing I want to do is take more fake Italian lessons.

"Here's your chance," says Marissa.

I turn to find Zara walking through the doorway to Marissa's office.

"I'll leave you two to chat," she says as she gets up and grabs her laptop.

I take a deep breath and hand Zara the paper to read. She laughs her way through it.

"Yeah, very funny," I say. "You just got me in trouble, and I don't have a post going up today because of you."

Zara pushes her lips together, clearly trying to

hold back another laugh. "I'm sorry. I was trying to teach you."

"How on earth is giving me the wrong words teaching me?" I ask.

"Wrong word, Skyler. It was one word. And will you ever forget that *più* means 'more'? Like, ever?" she challenges.

Darn it. She's totally right.

"My goodness, don't you fact-check?" she adds, scanning my post again.

I stand up and move closer to her. "Yes, I fact-check. That's why I wrote this one for you to see and another real one to send to Marissa."

Zara's eyebrows scrunch down. "So what's the problem?" she asks.

"The problem is that I sent the wrong one and now Marissa thinks I'm not capable of handling this job." I stand my ground.

"She said that?" asks Zara.

"No, but that was the gist of it," I answer.

"I'm really sorry, Skyler. How could I know you'd send in a fake post?" she asks.

Okay, well, she has me there. Although this never would have happened if she hadn't taught me the wrong word. I stand there, trying to figure out what to say next.

"I was going to tell you today if you hadn't figured it out by now," she says. "Clearly you don't like my methods." She looks down at the carpet, and I'm surprised by this rare moment of Zara not exuding confidence.

"Not really, no," I say.

When she finally meets my eyes, she actually looks a little hurt. "Okay, so do you want more Italian lessons or not?"

"Yes," I say. "I really want to learn Italian, so I don't have much of a choice."

But my sass doesn't work on Zara; she just gives it right back. "Sure you do, Skyler. It's not like I'm the only person in Italy who can teach you Italian," she says. "If you don't like the way I teach, find another tutor."

But I don't have time to search around for someone else, and I kind of want her to have to make up for what she did. "Marissa wants us to work this out," I say.

"Great. Then let's go outside and do this," says Zara.

I just had one of the best weekends of my life with my mom, and today starts with me having to spend more time with Zara. I check the hallways for any sign of Logan to at least make the day better, but no such luck.

I catch at least a little break, when Marissa and Logan end up in the same area outside where Zara and I are trying another Italian lesson.

"What are they doing?" Zara asks.

"No idea," I answer. "Probably planning some fabulous day in Venice while I'm stuck here with you."

Zara gives me an *I'm offended* look, but then she laughs. "Yeah, well, this is no picnic for me either. I'd much rather be going on whatever adventure they are."

The two of us are quiet as Logan and Marissa get up and walk away from the bench where they were sitting. Zara grabs my hand and yanks me up.

"Change of plans," she says. "Forget sitting here and memorizing vocabulary. You need to hear it being spoken." She pulls, and I jog along with her.

"Zara, where are we going?"

"*Dove,*" she says.

"Where is that?" I ask. She lets go of my hand, and I try to keep up with her as we head in the same direction as Marissa and Logan.

"It's not a place. It means 'where.' *Dove,*" she repeats.

She stops in front of me at the corner of the building and puts her arm out, stopping me from going any farther.

"Is that the *real* word?" I ask.

"Yes." She puts a finger over her lips and shushes me.

"Okay, so how do you say 'Why are we following Marissa and Logan' in Italian?" I whisper.

Zara turns to face me. "Because I like to have a little fun once in a while, and now that I can't teach you the wrong Italian words, I need to find a new way to make Italian lessons fun." She smiles a devious smile, but at least it seems genuine.

"And following them is fun?" I ask.

"We're only going to follow them for a little bit," she says. "And then we're going to just happen to run into them." She looks slyly around the corner.

"Wait a minute, do you like Logan?" It slips out of my mouth before I can think about the consequences.

Zara puts a hand on her hip. "Oh, come on. It's super obvious that *you* like Logan. So consider this a favor."

"What? No," I say, attempting to distract her from the point about Logan.

"You want the truth?" she asks.

I stare at her. "Of course I want the truth." Although I'm not sure I really do.

"Logan is my main competition for that school-year internship, and there's no way I'm letting him go off on some amazing day that he can write about while all I'll have to say in my post is that I taught you a few new words."

"Hey . . ." I pause to figure out what I'm most offended by in that statement. "What do you mean Logan is your main competition?"

"They're on the move." Zara grabs my hand again and leads me down the street, weaving our way through the crowds. "Shoot, they're getting on the bus. We need to make sure they don't see us."

"Zara, we're not supposed to be doing this.

We're only allowed to be unsupervised if we're in or near the office building. You know that," I say.

She gives me a look. "Do I really need to explain everything to you?"

I nod again, because obviously she does.

"We're not unsupervised if we're with Marissa," she says.

"But she doesn't know we're with her," I say. "And when we do run into them, how are we going to explain why we're there?"

Zara stops and pushes her lips together. "I don't know, but we'll figure it out. We have to get on that bus or we'll lose them."

This is a bad idea. A really, really bad idea. But I'm not about to let Zara think I'm a chicken on top of everything else she probably thinks of me.

"Okay, fine," I say. "We'll walk on with that tourist group and make sure we sit in the front, away from the aisle. Just lower your head when you get on the bus."

"Get your pass out," says Zara.

We scramble into the crowd of people and make our way to a seat without a problem.

"Hey, what did you mean by Logan being your

main competition?" I ask again, determined to get an answer this time.

Zara looks at me as if I'm supposed to know. I do, but I'm going to make her say it.

"Skyler, come on," she says. "Your first post was fine, but your second one isn't even being uploaded. Have you seen the number of comments Logan and I got on ours?"

"There are comments?" I ask.

"If you do it right, yeah," she says. "You have to post on all the social media sites and link to it to get more exposure. It's one of the things they look for, that you're engaging your audience."

"Engaging your audience," I repeat. "I guess I can't do that if I don't even have an audience because I have no posts. And now I don't have an Italian lesson to write about because you're dragging me on some weird spy mission."

Zara gives me a light smack on the shoulder. "Are you for real? *This* is your post, Skyler. You're in Venice, and you're going to learn some Italian today. You ready?"

I nod again.

"*Vincitore*. Winner," she says. "Only two of us

are going to win the internship, and if you want to have a shot at it, then you need to step it up and stop blaming me for everything."

She's right. "I so badly want to be a teen reporter for the travel magazine," I say. "Like, even more than I wanted to go out with Jake Middleton in sixth grade."

"*Did* you go out with Jake Middleton in sixth grade?" she asks.

I nod, and we both giggle like we're in sixth grade now.

"Sounds like you're a girl who knows what she wants and goes after it," says Zara. "I think we're more alike than either of us cares to admit."

Darn, she's right again.

Vincitore. Winner, I say in my head. Although I'm tempted to ask her how to say "loser" just in case.

"*Perdente,*" says Zara, quite possibly reading my mind. "Do you want to be a *vincitore* or a *perdente*?"

As she finishes her question, Marissa and Logan get off the bus. "Definitely a *vincitore,*" I say. "Let's go find out what *our* main competition is up to today."

ELEVEN

t turns out it's not as simple as following behind Marissa and Logan to their next location. Instead, we keep our distance as they walk to a booth to get tickets for a vaporetto, which is basically a Venetian water-bus.

"Come on, Zara. Enough is enough," I say. "We have no idea where they're going next."

She grabs my arm. "Not yet." She waits until Marissa leaves the ticket window and pulls me along with her. She says something in Italian to the ticket guy, pointing in Marissa's direction. "Quickly, please," she adds.

Zara grabs our tickets, and pulls me after her again until we find ourselves sneaking in line for the vaporetto, only a few people behind Marissa and Logan.

"How are we going to get on this boat without them seeing us?" I whisper.

"Skyler." Zara pauses and gives me a look. "We are perfectly capable of figuring this out. We're smart young women."

I'm not sure whether to thank her for the compliment or tell her she's out of her mind. Before I even get the chance to decide, the line moves and we move along with it.

"We need to get on the other side of the boat from them," I say. If I'm going to be a part of this, I might as well give my input. I've played enough hide-and-go-seek and have watched enough spy movies to at least know how to avoid being seen.

So as soon as Marissa and Logan head to the left, we head to the right and stand behind one of the partitions, but we stay where we can see them when they exit.

We cruise down the Grand Canal. I don't think I could ever get enough of the views of Venice. After ten minutes I almost forget we're on a mission. Almost.

Until Logan moves closer to where we're standing.

"Go, go, go," I whisper, pushing Zara toward the back of the boat. It's crowded enough that all we have to do is find a tall guy to hide behind.

When the boat stops, I hold on to the back of Zara's shirt to make sure we stay together in the crowd. We follow Marissa and Logan to St. Mark's Basilica, which I'd seen from afar on my weekend with Mom. The church is amazing from the outside. It's enormous and beautiful, with large mosaics and shiny gold figures at the top. The architecture here is incredible, and believe me, I never ever thought I'd be interested in architecture.

There's a really tall tower, and the square is lined with shops and people.

But what also stands out is all the pigeons. Whoa. I mean they are *everywhere*. If you're not bumping into a tourist, you're weaving your way through thousands of birds begging for food.

"What's with all these birds?" screeches Zara, waving her arms around her in what I'm guessing is an effort to keep them away. But it looks more like an odd dance she hasn't quite mastered, and I can't stop myself from laughing.

"I think they like you." I pull out my phone to record this for possible blackmail, but all Zara does is stand and stare at me. "Oh, come on. If we're going to be friends, I have to have some proof we actually have a good time together."

Zara flails her arms again as more birds scamper near her feet, and this time I catch it all on video. "I'm thinking of asking Marissa if I can do a video blog for my next assignment," I joke.

"Ha," says Zara. "That better not ever show up online, Skyler."

It's then that it hits me. "Oh, shoot! We lost them."

Zara stops shooing the birds away from her feet and scans the area. "There's no way we're going to find them again with all these people," she says.

But it turns out the girl is wrong every once in a while. I point at the entrance to the basilica. "No, wait. They're in line."

She sighs. "Well, that doesn't help us either. I'm not standing in line to see a church that Logan is already writing about."

"But that was our mission, right?" I say. "To find out what he's writing about? It turns out, it's nothing that's going to one-up us."

Zara tilts her head back and forth. "I guess so, but now what?"

"Now you teach me some more Italian," I say. "For starters, how do you say 'pigeon'?"

"*Come si dice*," she says.

I'm impressed with myself that I know what that means, because in Spanish class, when we wanted to ask "how do you say," we'd say *cómo se dice*. It sounds almost the same.

"Sorry, *come si dice* 'pigeon'?" I ask again.

"*Il piccione*," she answers.

I have no idea when I'll ever need to use that word in Italian, but I add it to my list of vocabulary anyway.

"Let's sit so you can listen," she says. "Tell me when you hear Italian being spoken."

I let out a chuckle, because of course I'm going to hear Italian being spoken. We're in Italy. But then I remember all the languages floating through the air. When we do sit, it isn't all that easy to find the Italian. I'm pretty sure I catch some German, Spanish, English with British accents, and definitely a Canadian or two.

"Them," I say, pointing subtly.

Zara nods. "Who else?"

I let the mash-up of languages float around me in big swirls, only understanding when I catch a bit of English. That is, until someone says *il piccione*, and I have to laugh. Turns out it *was* helpful to learn to say "pigeon" in Italian.

"See, I told you I'd teach you the real words this time," says Zara. "Here."

She pulls a list of words out of her pocket and hands it to me.

"You want me to learn these?" I ask.

"Yes. It's super important to know food words when you're eating in another country," she says. "Menus have some scary things on them."

I scan through the list. "Turnip greens? Seriously?"

"They put them in risotto sometimes. Do you want to learn Italian or not?" she asks.

"Who wants to learn Italian?" says a cute boy with an interesting accent standing in front of us. We both raise our hands like we're in class.

I give Zara a *You already know Italian* stare.

"Actually," she says quickly, "I speak fluent Italian. And Spanish. And a little Mandarin and Hindi."

Is this girl for real?

The boy holds out his hand. "I'm Gino Turay."

I lean forward. "Wait, do you know Marissa?" I ask.

"Skyler, just because they both live in Italy doesn't mean they know each other," says Zara.

"I know that. But they do have the same last name, so . . ." I wait for her to catch on.

"Yes, Marissa is my mother," Gino says. "And you must be the new interns I've heard so much about. Zara and Skyler, right?"

Zara and I look at each other and then turn back to Gino.

"Wait, how did you know that?" I ask.

Gino points to the DiBattisto logo at the top of the word list I'm holding. "It was an educated guess," he says.

Ah, gotcha.

"Your mom said she came here from the US a while ago," I say. "So I'm guessing you were born there?"

"Yeah, my dad is from Kenya, my mom is Italian, and I was born in the United States. So I'm really just your typical international man of mystery."

I let out a giggle and catch Zara giving him a googly-eyed look.

"Now that you know I'm not some strange Italian kid who wandered over here aimlessly, can I buy you ladies a coffee?" he asks. "The café here is ridiculously expensive, but the coffee is the best."

Well, who says no to that?

TWELVE

never drink coffee at home. But in Italy it's everywhere, so when in Venice . . .

"Are you here with my mom?" asks Gino. "I'm supposed to find her, actually."

I elbow Zara to answer, since she's the one who got us here in the first place.

"She's around here somewhere," says Zara.

Gino waits, but Zara doesn't elaborate and neither do I.

"Okay, being cryptic," he says. "That works for me. So do you really want to learn Italian, Skyler?"

"I do," I answer. "Zara has been teaching me,

but so far I pretty much know how to order more dessert and how to say 'pigeon.'"

He shakes his head. "Well, you never know when those will come in handy," he says.

"I'm writing some of my blog posts on learning Italian," I say. "I'd love to have some extra help if you're offering."

Zara furrows her eyebrows. "Hey," she says, elbowing me this time, "I am an excellent teacher."

"Keep telling yourself that," I say. "Besides, you were right. You said it should be easy to find someone to teach me Italian in Italy, and well, would you look at that." I motion toward Gino and take a moment to smirk at Zara's expression. "I mean, since you already know, like, ten languages, you don't need lessons."

"Three," she says. "And some Mandarin."

"Right, some Mandarin."

"And some Hindi," she adds.

Gino is paying no attention to us, sipping his cappuccino like we're not subtly fighting over who gets to spend time with him.

"My mom was trying to get me to do some tutoring," he says. "Turns out my schedule just opened up."

I cannot even describe the feeling I get when he looks at me. I bite my lip, but it does nothing to contain my smile. I don't even care that Zara is giving me a jealous stare.

"When do you need to meet up with my mom?" asks Gino.

I still haven't quite recovered from his attention. "Well, we, um . . . We're taking the vaporetto back on our own. We have it mastered now. What about you?"

"My mom left her flash drive at home, so I offered to run it over to her." He looks around the square. "I was supposed to text her when I got here."

"Well, we should go and let you meet up with her, then," says Zara, tugging on my shirt. "Hey, can you not mention that you saw us? We were supposed to be back at the office a while ago."

"Sure. How about if we meet tomorrow for a lesson?" Gino asks me.

I want to shout that I'd love to, but Marissa already scheduled a day to go with me to collect some stories for my other blog posts, just like she's doing today with Logan. And I really need a winner of a post right about now. "I can't tomorrow, maybe Wednesday?"

"Wednesday's good," says Zara.

I shake my head in disbelief at this girl.

"Technically, you're my student, so I'll need to oversee these sessions with Gino," she says.

Gino isn't fazed by any of this, or maybe he's just not paying attention. He takes my phone and punches his number in my contacts. "Give me a call."

As soon as he's out of sight, Zara let's me have it. "You are not going off with that boy on your own."

"Going off with that boy?" I repeat. "We'll probably meet outside the office, like you and I were supposed to. I think someone is a bit jealous."

Zara is nothing at all like Ella, but I'm reminded that being opposites in a lot of ways doesn't mean you won't be the best of friends. Although I can't even imagine being the best of anything with Zara.

"We need to get back to the boat stop," she says. "I think it's this way."

"Hold on." I stop. I consider *not* saying what I'm about to say, but decide it's time to maybe enjoy this little adventure. "I know I've been complaining about this, but since we're here, don't you think we should take a look around?" I put my arms out and do a dramatic spin.

She laughs. "I guess we do have some time if they're touring the church. Are you saying you're actually up for having some fun?"

"Yes," I say. "I think I am."

While I'm happy to stay where we are and check out all the shops, Zara wants to walk outside the tourist area.

I shouldn't just follow her without another thought, but I do. As soon as we cross bridges over canal after canal, I can't even remember which direction we came from, let alone where we're heading. It's quieter than back at the square.

"Zara, do you have any idea where we are?" I ask.

She pauses and does a complete turn. "Yes. It's, uh, this way."

I follow her again, not so confident this time.

She stops, turns, and goes back the direction we came.

"Zara!" I call from behind her.

"I don't have a clue, okay?" she says. "This place is all bridges and boats and the buildings are starting to look the same and I don't know which way to go next."

Great. Because I certainly don't either. "We need to head toward the water, right?" But even as I say it, I know what Zara's response will be.

"Which water, Skyler? There's water everywhere in this city!"

I take out my phone to use the GPS, but I can't get a signal.

"Don't bother," says Zara. "There's something about all the tall buildings and the narrow streets that can throw it off."

I push my lips together and try to think. "We could ask someone."

"We're not asking anyone," says Zara.

"Why not? We're lost. When people are lost, they ask for directions."

"We're not lost, we're just temporarily out of whack," she says.

"Seriously?" I say. "That's not a thing."

"It's a thing."

I'm tempted to leave her here, except the only thing worse than being lost in Venice is being lost in Venice by myself. I'm stuck with her. "Not a thing, Zara. We're lost."

POSTCARDS FROM VENICE

"Or . . . ," she says, "we're on an adventure."

I'm always the one back home who's up for an adventure. It's a little weird to be the more timid one now. I guess being in a new, unfamiliar place will do that. So will being with Zara.

This *could* count as an adventure, though. But we're going to have to work together to figure it out. "Yeah, okay," I say. "If you're up for it."

I get something more than a smirk from her, although I can't verify that it's a smile.

There's a lot of "this way" and "that way" and "I think I remember that building" until things start to look more familiar. But halfway across one of the bridges Zara spins around and pushes me back to the other side in a hurry.

"What are you doing?" I ask.

"Shh." She puts her finger over her lips and guides me into a doorway.

"Zara, what's going on?" I peek my head around the corner, but all I see is a couple of older men standing on the bridge, facing our way. "Do you know them?" I ask.

She pulls me back. "It's Marissa's husband," she whispers.

"How do you know that?" I ask.

"He's friends with my aunt. That's how I got a spot in the mentorship program."

"Great. Should we ask him how to get back to the vaporetto stop?" I say.

"He'll tell Marissa," answers Zara.

I check the time on my phone. "We're going to get in even bigger trouble if we don't get back before Marissa and Logan," I say. "We've been out here awhile."

"We can do this, Skyler," she says. "Don't give up yet."

We both peek around the corner, and this time the bridge is empty.

"It's clear," says Zara. "Let's go!"

We step out onto the street, but I stop. She turns around. "What?"

"Is this some kind of trick again?" I ask. "Because I'm not writing about this. I'm not writing about getting lost and ruining another post."

"*Perso? No!*" says Zara. "*Esplorando? Sì!*"

Pear-so. That's how I visualize the word in my head.

"Translation?" I ask.

"Lost? No. Exploring? Yes!"

Well, I hate to admit it, but that's actually

brilliant. I might regret this (and will definitely be fact-checking), but I let it out anyway. "Okay, I kind of love that," I say. "Maybe I can use it as the title for my next post?"

Zara laughs and gives me a light smack on the shoulder. "Except you can't admit you were wandering around Venice today or we'll get in trouble, remember?"

"So how will we explain meeting Gino if we weren't in Venice?" I ask.

"Well, Skyler," says Zara, "I guess it's about time you decided whether or not you want to be a storyteller. You'll come up with something."

She walks over the bridge and I follow, because this adventure isn't over just yet.

THIRTEEN

When we get to the ticket booth, it's clear we were gone long enough for Marissa and Logan to have toured the church—and to have made it back to the vaporetto.

"Go!" I whisper-yell to Zara, pushing her behind a group of tourists.

"What are you doing?" she asks, begrudgingly going where I guide her.

"We took too long," I say. "They're here." We both lean to the side, and I point to Marissa and Logan, who are already in line for the vaporetto.

"We'll never get back before them," says Zara. "And we clearly can't get on that boat."

I take a deep breath. "So now what?" I ask.

But Zara doesn't seem to have a solution.

"We're going to be in serious trouble," I say. "What if we get kicked off the internship?"

Zara just stands there, staring at me. She takes a deep breath. "My parents will flip out if that happens. *I'll* flip out if I lose my chance for the school-year position." She grips her hands together. It's the first time I've seen her even the slightest bit nervous. "We have to find another way to get back."

"There isn't one," I say. "It's too far to walk. We should go admit what we did and face the consequences."

Zara shakes her head. "You don't understand, Skyler. If Marissa tells my aunt I went off on my own, I won't see the light of day until next year. At the earliest."

I try to gauge if the situation is as bad as she's making it out to be. I mean, my mom will most certainly be disappointed, but I'll mostly get a lecture, which, honestly, I deserve.

"We either come clean or we get in more trouble when they get back and can't find us," I say. "Come on."

I grab Zara's arm and pull her along with me. "Marissa!" I shout.

Marissa has a very surprised look on her face and immediately gets out of line when she sees the two of us. She scans the people around us as if she's checking to see if there's an adult here before she decides how to handle this.

Now she's just standing there, clearly waiting for us to speak first. The silence is nerve-wracking.

"We followed you," I spit out, not able to stand her stare one second longer. "We're really sorry."

Behind her, Logan clenches his teeth in a *yikes* sort of way. Zara stays quiet as Marissa looks at her.

"And whose idea was that?" asks Marissa.

Zara and I turn to look at each other. Until now I'd mostly just seen the confidence in her eyes. The girl who wanted this internship so badly, but also dared to venture off the beaten path. The girl from all over, with a rebel streak bigger than mine's ever been.

But now there's fear in her eyes. Maybe regret. Possibly even a bit of pleading.

"It was a really bad idea, and we're sorry." I keep the whole thing as vague as possible and hope Marissa doesn't even realize I'm not answering her question.

Marissa looks from me to Zara. "Why would you do that?" she asks. "You could have just asked to come along."

Zara turns to me, suddenly seeming so vulnerable. I can't throw her under the bus.

"I know," I say. "We just wanted some adventure."

Marissa turns back to the boat, which is almost done loading. "Do you have tickets?" she asks.

Zara and I nod.

"Let's go, then," says Marissa. "We'll deal with this when we get back."

As we board the boat, I don't know who I want to avoid more: Marissa, Zara, or Logan.

Marissa leads me directly to Mom's office and then takes Zara upstairs to call her aunt. I should be focused on my own situation, but I can't stop worrying about what's going to happen with Zara.

"I'm very disappointed," says Mom. I sit across from her desk with my head down. "Did I really need to tell you not to go off on your own in a foreign country?"

"No," I answer. "I knew better. I'm sorry."

"I have a ton of work to do, Skyler. You know

I'm trying to get an extended contract," she says. "I don't have time for this."

And there it is. Mom has been so much more attentive than usual, but I knew work would eventually come first again.

"You never have time," I say. I quickly realize this is not the place to have this conversation, and it didn't come out in a very respectful tone. "I'm sorry, Mom. I didn't mean it like that."

Mom gets up from her desk and sits next to me. "Listen, I know I still have a long way to go to make things up to you, but I'm trying. Even if it might not always look like it." She puts her arm around me and pulls me in for a sideways hug. We sit for a few minutes without saying a word. "But none of that makes it okay to wander off by yourselves."

I nod. "What consequences do I get?" I ask, wanting to get this over with.

"I really do have to get back to work," she says. "Call your father and tell him what happened. I'll leave it up to him."

With Mom working all the time, decisions have always gone to Dad. In a way, I'm relieved to get back to the way it usually works in our family. But

Dad is in a whole other country, and she's letting him decide my punishment? She couldn't step up and take care of this herself?

"I'll call now." I get up and head for the door, and I don't look back. Realizing Mom is still not putting me first is enough of a consequence.

FOURTEEN

As requested, I meet Marissa outside the office the next morning. I'm ready to face whatever consequence she'll be giving me for my lack of judgment.

"Good morning," she says.

"Good morning." I jump right in. "I'm really sorry I made such bad choices yesterday. It won't happen again."

Marissa has a kind smile, but she's no pushover. "I believe you," she says. "Which is why I've decided that whatever punishment you received from your parents is acceptable to me. Although it will be a factor when I decide on the internships."

"I understand," I say. "What about Zara?" I can't stop wondering how she's doing.

"Her parents canceled a Paris trip they'd been planning with her," she says. "But her aunt is allowing her to continue the summer internship."

Yikes. I suddenly feel lucky that all Dad took away was three weeks' allowance.

"She never sees them to begin with," I say. Because I can't even imagine not seeing my parents all the time. It's hard enough being here without my dad.

Marissa stops being all business for a minute, and her face softens. "I know. But it's not our place to interfere."

I take a deep breath and let it out in one loud exhale.

"Okay, then," says Marissa. "I have a big day planned for us, so let's start with a clean slate, shall we?"

"I'd really like that," I say. "Thank you."

We take the train to Venice and then hop on the vaporetto line 3 to Murano. But since I have never even heard of Murano before, I have no choice but to ask Marissa where we're going and show her once again how little I know about this place.

"So . . . why are we going to Murano specifically?" I ask, hoping she'll spill all the details.

"Because you wanted stories," answers Marissa.
The boat zooms through the Venetian Lagoon as
the sun shines overhead. "Today you'll meet people
with stories worth writing about."

"And they're in Murano?" I ask.

"Some of them," she answers. "Do you know
what Murano is famous for?"

Oh man, how I wish I did. But I have nothing to
impress her with other than a guess. "Food?"

Marissa laughs. "Well, of course. This is Italy.
But Murano is also known for its glass."

Hmm, this I can use.

"Oh, wow, I actually find glassmaking really
fascinating," I say, trying to throw in a big, writer
kind of word. "I've been to the Corning Museum
of Glass back home in New York. It's really cool."
So much for my one-word streak. Now I'm back to
words like "cool."

"I'm happy to hear that," says Marissa. "Because
I'm getting you a backstage tour." The boat gets
a bit loud as we ride over some waves. Marissa
pauses and leans in. "Most of the glass shops are
filled with tourists, but some of them prefer not

to showcase their craft. Those are the best ones to see."

The boat slows down as we near the dock. "Do we get to see them?" I ask.

"We sure do," answers Marissa.

The first thing I notice when we get to Murano is all the boats. They're different shapes and sizes, but most of them come to a point like the tip of a shovel. There are normal things happening here— moms with kids, old men walking slowly, friends chatting endlessly—but it's still like I'm in another world. The beautiful sidewalks that run along the canals, the green and beige awnings along the way, and the faded pastel colors of the buildings— yellows and reds and pinks, but mostly clay-orange and white. Marissa says the buildings in Burano— another island in the lagoon—are much brighter, with vibrant colors all over the place. I add it to my list of places to see.

There are outdoor stands selling anything a tourist could want, but it's when we get away from the water and onto the narrow streets that we pass restaurants with outdoor seating, little cafés crowded with customers, and shops selling scarves and jewelry and bags that say VENEZIA. We peek into some of the shops and cafés as we walk along, and not once does Marissa rush me, which is awesome.

"Here we are," says Marissa as we walk up to another glass shop. "Get your notepad ready. You're about to meet Daniela." She walks through the door to the shop, and all I can do is wonder what exactly I should be ready for.

Daniela ushers us into the glass shop with a big Italian welcome. The storefront is amazing, with glass candleholders and chandeliers and vases of all different colors. I'm careful not to touch or even breathe on anything if I can help it.

"You make all of this?" I ask.

"Yes. Would you like to see how?" asks Daniela.

I nod fast little nods and follow her and Marissa into the back. Maybe if writing doesn't go well, I could be a glassmaker. Might as well keep a running list of possibilities.

I get introduced to the people in the shop, and each one of them explains a little more about how all of this is done. There are long rods and what looks like an old-time oven with what must be a very hot flame. I stand here in awe as they melt and twist and turn the glass until it becomes a beautiful dish that will probably sit in the middle of a fancy table, covered with fruit or the best kinds of chocolates. I don't even know how long we've been standing here, but I'm mesmerized.

I'm also pretty sure this is not a talent I have.

"I could never do something like this," I say.

But Daniela is quick to correct me. "It is a skill for sure," she says. "But it takes time and training and a careful and patient hand. No one can do this the first time." She points to the dish that was just made.

I smile, acknowledging that yes, of course, anything takes training and practice. I'm certainly learning that with this internship.

We go to an office upstairs, and Marissa guides me to sit down in one of the comfy chairs. I get out my notebook and a pen.

"Marissa tells me you have some questions for me," says Daniela.

Questions? Yikes. I thought I was here to collect stories, not ask questions.

Marissa must sense my hesitation, because she

puts a hand on mine and speaks up. "Skyler is new to reporting, so why don't we start with a little about you and we'll go from there."

Daniela is definitely not shy. She opens up about her childhood, the homes she's lived in, how she met her husband . . . I write furiously as she talks, with no time to think about which part of it I want to focus on or to ask questions. My brain can't keep up, my hand can't jot it down fast enough, and on top of all that, my stomach lets out an enormous growl.

I put a hand on my abdomen like that will quiet it down. "Oh, I'm sorry," I say. "Ever since we got to Italy and tasted the food, it's like my stomach has a mind of its own."

Daniela laughs, gets up from her chair, and leaves the room.

"Marissa, I don't know if I'm cut out for this." I glance at my notes, which are all over the paper. I can barely read anything. "I don't know how I'm going to turn this into a blog post. It's a mess."

She turns in the chair so she's facing me. "For one thing, remember that this is a social media internship. Take a few photos. All you need for those are captions."

She's right. I keep forgetting the simpler part of this assignment.

"Okay, right," I say. "But what about the interview?"

Marissa takes the notepad from me. "Have you been listening?" she asks.

"What do you mean?"

"I see that you can write things down. It appears you've had some experience taking notes. But are you a good listener?" she asks.

I laugh, thinking about how my teachers would answer that question. "I guess I'm a good listener when I'm talking with my friends," I answer.

"Okay, so think of Daniela as one of your friends telling you a story," she says. "The important thing is that you hear her. What she's really saying. That's where you'll get your story from."

Daniela comes back in the room carrying a big glass plate of cheese, crackers, and fruit. The grapes are draped around the edge like a piece of artwork.

"Now, where was I?" she asks, sitting back down.

"You were telling us about your trip through Italy and what inspired you to get into the glass business," I remind her.

"Oh, right," says Daniela. She pushes the plate of food closer to me. "What a wonderful listener you are."

Marissa and I smile at each other, because maybe, just maybe, I've got this.

FIFTEEN

Dear Ella,

Hi! I have SO much to tell you. I don't even know where to begin.

I have two blog posts to work on, *"Perso? No! Esplorando? Sì!"* (Lost? No! Exploring? Yes!) and "A Glassmaker's Tale." Luckily, I finished "The Part of Venice You Don't Want to See" right after we went on that creepy adventure. I'm still waiting to see what Marissa thinks of it.

Oh, wait, you wouldn't have gotten the postcard yet! Well, let me tell you what I did.

I haven't heard from Ella in a week, but I know she's busy. It's summertime, after all. Still, I need to talk to her one way or another, so I keep sending her e-mails.

After a few more minutes go by I stop and remind myself that I need to focus on work. If I can get the posts done quickly, that'll give me more time with Gino today for our Italian lesson at the office. Marissa was thrilled to find out we'd met and that he'd agreed to help. Although she wasn't as thrilled to find out we'd met on our unapproved adventure.

But getting my posts done quickly is not an easy task. Especially when the phone rings.

"Hello?" Everybody texts these days, but I have to admit, sometimes it's so much easier just to chat.

"Hey, it's Logan. I didn't get to see you yesterday, so I thought I'd check in," he says.

Does that mean he missed me? Whoa.

"I went to Murano with Marissa," I respond.

"I heard," he says. "For the record, I'm glad you didn't get kicked off the internship."

And *I'm* glad he can't see me smiling through the phone.

"Today is a writing day for me," says Logan. "I have a couple posts I want to finish. Want to work together?"

I stop myself from yelling, *Yes, I do!* "Sure. I have some drafts to edit too. Where?"

Logan calls to someone in the background, but it's muffled. "How about the conference room at the office? Marissa says it's okay. She's doing something with Zara today."

I'm happy Zara is still allowed to do the internship, but I'm also excited that it'll just be me and Logan.

"My mom and I are heading in soon, so I'll meet you there," I say. "I just need to stop and get a few postcards first."

"Great idea," he says. "They're a lost art, if you ask me."

As I close my laptop and tuck it in its sleeve, I make a mental note to pick up a couple extra postcards for Logan so he can write home. I try to hide my smile as I head in for breakfast, but apparently I don't do such a good job.

"Well, good morning," says Mom. "Big plans today?"

Mom and I seem to be past our awkward

moment from the other day, so I figure there's no point bringing it up. I sit at the table, where there's already a plate of toast and fruit waiting for me. Mom cooking is a new thing, so I pick at the food slowly, even if it is something as simple as heating up bread.

"I'm meeting Logan to catch up on our posts," I say.

Mom stops stirring her coffee. "I thought you were meeting Gino for an Italian lesson?"

"Oh, shoot. I double-booked," I say mid-bite.

Mom laughs. It's really nice to see her so happy and relaxed. "Sweetie, you're much too young to be double-booking your dates."

"Mom! They're not dates," I insist. "One is to write and the other is to learn Italian."

Mom is back to stirring her coffee. "Well, as long as we've gotten that sorted out, we need to make a plan for dinner. Looks like I'll be working late."

I slump my shoulders and pick at my toast, try-ing (unsuccessfully) to hide my disappointment.

Mom immediately picks up on my attitude shift. "Skyler . . ." She doesn't say anything else.

It's quiet, and in this moment the world isn't swirling around me. There's nowhere to be and no deadlines for Mom to meet. In this moment I get to have her all to myself. But as soon as one of us speaks, the bubble will pop. It'll be back to the real world, where I miss my mom, even when she's right in front of me.

I focus on my breakfast, and my mind goes back to my more immediate issue. Because when I get that teen reporter job, she'll be the one missing *me* instead. I send a text to Gino.

Have to write. Free tomorrow?

He responds immediately. **Sure. See you in the morning.**

Well, that wasn't so bad. Until I get another text.

Might go with my mom and Zara today, then. Good luck!

Oh, Zara is just going to love this, and I'll have to hear about it for sure. But at least I get to meet up with Logan, and I'll make sure she hears about *that*.

What I'm supposed to be doing: Writing my blog posts.

What I'm actually doing: Alternating between staring into space and finishing my e-mail to Ella. It's been a week since I've heard from her, which feels like such a long time. So instead of getting started on my exploring post (or even the one about my trip to Murano), I'm letting myself get distracted.

Writing to Ella isn't like putting a post together. There's no planning or rewording. I don't have to think about what Marissa will say or how many comments it might get once it's up. There's no need to make sure I have the right balance of informative, yet funny.

I just write.

I describe the city of Venice with all its little streets and bridges and canals. I tell her about the people I've met—careful to turn my screen away from Logan as I write about him. I upload some pictures from my adventures. I write about how wonderful it's been to spend time with my mom. Because Ella will understand.

I'm completely lost in another world until Logan's voice stops my session with his adorable accent.

"How's it coming over there?" he asks. "You've been typing furiously for an hour."

I hadn't even realized how long I'd spent on the e-mail—or how long the e-mail had gotten, for that matter.

"Oh, sorry, yeah, I'm getting a lot done," I say,

not sure whether or not Logan would approve of *what* I'm getting done. I remind myself that he's my competition. Not that I see him that way at all.

"Your post is up," he says, turning his laptop toward me. "It just went live this morning, and you already have some comments."

I'd forgotten it was my day on the company blog, but when I see the title "The Part of Venice You Don't Want to See" along with my name underneath, I smile.

"Really? There are already comments?" I ask, leaning in and scrolling down the page. I had no idea they were even important, but according to Zara, they're a big factor in Marissa's decision on who gets to continue. "I should post on social media, right? And link to it?"

"That's what I'd do," he says, his hair flopping forward the tiniest bit.

"I'm not sure I'm cut out for this writing thing," I admit out loud. "But is it weird that at the same time I kind of feel like I have a talent for it and it's been in there this whole time waiting for me to use it?"

"Not at all," says Logan. "You must get top-notch grades back home," he says.

I cannot stop the laugh that escapes my mouth. "Not quite, but thank you," is what I manage to spit out. I'm that kid who's always somewhere between a great student and a not-so-great student, getting by and calling it a day. But teachers like me. They say I have a "positive energy," so I'm at least on the right track, I guess.

But this writing thing, when it's not an assignment in English and people are actually reading my words and commenting? It's kind of awesome.

"Logan, can I ask you something?"

"Go for it," he says.

"Is it wrong of me to even go after this internship?" I ask. "I might not even be here for the school year, and I'm clearly not as good as you and Zara." I bite my lip, not convinced I want an answer.

"You're a good writer, Skyler," he says. "Just keep at it."

I'm pretty sure the words "you're a good writer, Skyler" have never been spoken. Not by a teacher, not by my parents, and certainly not by a cute Australian boy sitting across from me at a conference table in Italy.

Logan stands up and closes his laptop. "I want to show you something." He waits for me at the door and holds out his hand, which, okay, makes me move a little faster.

He takes my hand and leads me through a bunch of cubicles, down a hallway, and into the break room.

"You're hungry?" I ask. "It's not even lunchtime."

Logan smiles and opens up a set of doors I hadn't noticed before. When he does, a beautiful balcony comes into view.

"Can we go out there?" I ask.

"Of course."

We step onto the balcony, and I'm quickly reminded of where I am. Not stuck in an office building doing something I don't want to be doing, but in a place where all I have to do is open a window or a door and outside is . . . Italy.

"I hope you're here for the school year," says Logan. "And if you beat me out for that internship or you get Marissa's recommendation for the teen reporter spot, I will still write, because I love it. Because whether I'm in Australia or Italy or, I don't know, on the moon, I will still want to write and I'll find some way to do it."

I admire his dedication and enthusiasm, but I'm not sure I have the same things in me. "I think I like to write," I answer.

Logan gives me a look. "I know you weren't writing your posts back there, Skyler," he says. "But whatever you *were* writing, it made you happy."

I tap the railing with the toe of my shoe and watch it like it's the most interesting event in the world. "I was writing to my friend," I finally say, summoning up the courage to look him in the eye.

"That counts too," he says. "I mean, come on, you spent an hour writing instead of texting. That's pretty big."

We both laugh and turn to the view of the street, of the piazza, of the people going about their day. I see one man in particular who's sweeping in front of a café, singing and doing little dance steps as he turns the broom, like he couldn't be happier if he tried. I want to know more about him. I want to hear his story.

"You're right," I answer. "Hey, I know I'm already two blog posts behind, but would you come with me to go collect a story?"

Without another word, we're heading back down the hallway, checking in with our parents, and walking out the main doors.

SIXTEEN

Neither Logan nor I speak Italian, so I'm crossing my fingers as we approach the dancing shopkeeper.

"Excuse me," I say, trying to get his attention. "Do you speak English?"

The man stops sweeping and smiles. "Yes. I am Patrizio." He holds out his hand, and I shake it. He points up at the sign that reads DA PATRIZIO.

"I'm Skyler and this is my friend Logan."

Patrizio turns to Logan and shakes his hand.

"We're interns"—I point across the street at the office building—"and we write blog posts about Italy and its people."

Patrizio is totally focused on what I'm saying, broom in hand.

"We were, well, I was wondering if maybe we could chat with you for a bit," I say. All the newness of Italy has made my usually get-out-there-and-talk-to-everyone self a little hesitant, but today I'm getting back to being me.

"Of course, my dear." He says something in Italian to the people sitting at the closest outside table. They take their things and get up from their seats, all with a smile. "Please, sit."

He pulls out a chair for me and motions for Logan to sit down across from me, then takes the last chair for himself.

"What can I do for you?" asks Patrizio.

I pull a notepad and pencil out of my bag, hoping he's got a good story for us. I need a good story.

"Would you tell us about yourself?" I ask.

Patrizio smiles and leans back in the chair. "I will start at the beginning," he says. "It was 1932 ..."

Wow, he wasn't kidding. Patrizio starts with the day he was born, and I manage to calculate his age pretty quickly. When someone from inside calls out to him, he excuses himself for a minute.

I lean over toward Logan and whisper, "Oh my goodness, no way is this guy eighty-six! Did you see him dancing?"

Logan's wide eyes tell me he can't believe it either. "I hope I'm that happy and full of energy at eighty-six."

I smile at the way he says the age, like "*ay*-tee seeks."

"What?" asks Logan.

I bite my whole bottom lip to attempt to stop my smile, but no luck. Spit it out, Skyler. Where's the get-out-there-and-talk-to-everyone Skyler I just said I was going to be?

"Nothing," I respond. But when Logan crosses his arms, I know I'm not getting out of it that easily. "Okay, fine. I freaking love your accent, all right? It's awesome. I mean, it is the best accent I have ever heard in real life." I take a deep breath.

Now Logan can't stop smiling. "Real life?" he says. "Have you heard a better one in the movies?"

OMG, I haven't. I shake my head.

Thank goodness Patrizio is back before I have to admit it out loud, though.

He sets two plates down in front of us. "You have had mozzarella in carrozza?" he asks.

Logan and I shake our heads.

"You try," he says, inching the plates toward us.

I take a bite and can't believe how delicious it is. It's like a deep-fried mozzarella sandwich. "Patrizio, this is the best thing ever!"

He nods slowly with a big smile on his face. "Now, where were we?" he asks, but he's not really looking for an answer. Even in his eighties, this guy is sharp as a tack. "So in 1932 . . ."

I set down my food and furiously take notes, picturing Marissa on my shoulder encouraging me to listen to the story. Across the table Logan takes another notepad and pen from my bag, mouthing, *I'll take notes too*. He must see me struggling to keep up.

I never knew that listening was truly an art. You have to decide what to note and then write it down at lightning speed so you can remember it all. Maybe even use a direct quote or two. I have not yet mastered this skill, but I'm trying.

"Then in 1943 . . ." Patrizio isn't done yet. After I finish this blog post, I'm pretty sure I'll be able to write his life story into a full-length biography.

Logan gives me a thumbs-up, and I let myself take a three-second break to smile at him before Patrizio gets to the 1950s.

Logan and I plop down on a bench outside the office. I'm exhausted.

"How does listening and taking notes suck so much energy out of you?" I ask.

"I don't know," answers Logan, "but that guy has had the most interesting life of anyone I've ever met. How'd you know to pick him?"

I glance across the street where Patrizio is now behind the counter chatting with one of the customers. "It was something about him," I say. "The way he danced and sang like he didn't have a care in the world."

I flip through my pages and pages of notes.

"How is it that he's lived seventy-three years more than me, has been through big things and little things and everything in between, and yet I'm the one who's stressed out at thirteen years old? Something about that isn't right."

Logan leans back. "It is a bit out of whack, isn't it? We could learn a lot from him."

We sit in silence, and I imagine Logan is

thinking the same things I am. Trying to process everything we just heard. The stories, and the way Patrizio told them with such emotion and detail.

"Hey, there." My mom's voice knocks me out of my thoughts.

"Oh, hi, Mom," I say.

"Hi, Mrs. G." Logan stands up and offers her the bench.

"How's it coming?" she asks.

"It's sort of coming along great, and I'm also kind of behind at the same time," I say. "I have a million ideas, but none of them are written."

"Well, how about if I take you both to lunch and then you can get back to work after that?" asks Mom.

I'm a little surprised that she's out of the office in the middle of the day, and my shock seems to freeze my tongue in place.

Logan kicks at my shoe and nods toward my mom.

"I'd love to, Mom, but we actually just ate," I say.

"Oh," she says. "Dessert, then? I'll just grab some lunch for myself."

"That would be ace," says Logan.

"Yeah, I'm not turning *that* down," I say.

Mom laughs. "Would you mind if we go to Patrizio's?" she asks. "It's one of my favorite places. You absolutely have to try the mozzarella in carrozza sometime."

I simply smile as Mom grabs my hand and we walk across the street together with Logan close behind.

SEVENTEEN

Dear Ella,

Answers below in mint green (of course). It's
weird being a world away and not knowing
what's happening with you. So it's your turn.
What's going on with Alex? Are you excited
to start at a new school? What have I missed
while I'm over here eating gelato?

I totally meant to get back to writing my blog
posts after lunch, but there was an e-mail from
Ella in my in-box. She must have written back
the second she got up this morning. I opened it as
soon as I saw the subject line: *Tell me everything!*

It was full of questions like:

What's going on with Logan?

What's next on the list?

Do you know if you're staying in Italy?

So I changed the font color and answered every question in mint green:

Nothing.

Not sure.

Not yet.

But as I look over my responses now, I realize I haven't given her much information (unlike this morning's e-mail to her), so I go back and elaborate. Then I ask her more of my own questions.

I know she probably won't write back right away, but I stare at my computer screen anyway, missing home a little bit. Okay, maybe a lot. And even though I'm not quite sure we'd be hanging out together if I were there, missing Ella.

I pull my laptop screen down low enough to see that Logan is hard at work. He gives his keyboard a big tap with his pointer finger and leans back in his chair across the table from me.

"Aaaaand, done," he says. "Post number seven, *finito*."

"You're done with your *seventh* post?" I ask.

"But it's only been a little over a week, and we still have until next Friday to get all of them finished."

"I like to get things done early," he says. "Bad habit my parents instilled in me." His sarcastic smile is totally adorable.

While I'm secretly panicking inside that now I'm way, way behind in the interns race, I can't help but get all flirty right back. I guess the real Skyler is still in there somewhere.

"Well, I think it's an admirable trait," I say, leaning on the table. My phone goes off before I can really turn on the charm.

A text from Gino.

Are we still on for an Italian lesson tomorrow?

I eye my computer screen. My totally blank computer screen. Logan is on post number seven, and Zara's probably well into double digits just to earn extra credit. I've finished exactly three posts. Three.

Ugh. Can't. I have a TON of writing to do.

So far only one of my post ideas has to do with learning Italian, and I'd planned to write at least two more, so I text again.

Maybe Friday?

I add a smiley-face emoji to make sure he knows I still very much want his help. *Need* his help.

When I look up again, Logan is gone, but all of his stuff is still here. It's easy to spot his backpack with the Australian flag on the side. I wish I knew more about Australia. I probably should have paid more attention in social studies. But who knew I'd be trying to impress a sweet Australian boy someday? They should really mention that possibility in class.

I desperately need to get back to work. I figure I can at least plan out the last of my topics.

I tap my fingers on the table.

I spin around in my chair.

I fiddle with my ponytail.

Oh, come on, Skyler!

I'm already distracted, so I pull up the company blog to see if I have any more comments now that I've learned how to cross-post on social media.

Except my post isn't up top anymore. Zara's next one is.

And OMG, it gets even worse! The title?

"Perso? No! Esplorando? Sì!"

"She seriously stole my idea?!" I stand up and pound on the table as Logan walks back into the room with a bunch of snack bags.

"Everything okay in here?" asks Logan.

"No," I say. "It is definitely not okay. Zara not only stole my idea, but she also somehow managed to worm her way into my scheduled day so my post got bumped."

I can't stand still, so I pace the room. All I can think is that instead of having to come up with three more ideas, I have to come up with four.

"How'd she do that?" asks Logan.

"I have no idea," I say, still pacing. "She probably talked her way around the rules, and Marissa fell for her sweet little charade. But I'll tell you what, I am not falling for it again."

Logan slowly drops the snacks on the table and keeps his distance.

"I'm sorry," I say. "I thought we were actually getting along and now she has me all riled up and I'm already behind and I don't know if I can do this."

Logan comes around the table and sits down in front of me. "Skyler, we just spent all morning getting just about the best stories ever told on this earth. If you want to do this, you have the information you need to write an amazing post."

I wonder for a split second if Logan would ever

take his notes and steal Patrizio's story from me. But I don't wonder for very long.

"You've been writing like crazy this afternoon," he says. "You must have a pretty solid post to turn in by now?"

I don't say a word.

"Oh, come on. You haven't been working on your posts since we got back from lunch?" he asks.

I shake my head.

"What have you been doing the whole time?"

"Writing to my friend Ella again." I sit down in the chair next to him, rotating it a quarter turn. Just enough so he can't see my face.

"I've been trying to give you pep talks, but honestly, it's like you've convinced yourself you can't do this," says Logan. He stands up, and I force myself to face him.

"I don't know what I want," I say. "I mean, I want that teen reporter job, but maybe not for the right reasons. I like telling stories, but then why can't I write? Why can't I stay on top of my deadlines?"

Logan shrugs. "I think you need to figure all of that out, Skyler. If you decide you need my help, you know where to find me."

He walks around the table and packs up his

things, tossing one of the bags of chips my way and waving on his way out.

I sit here, with a million things to do and no motivation to do them. Chances are I'm leaving in a couple weeks anyway. Maybe I should step back and let Zara and Logan duke it out for first place.

Ha. Let them. Like I'm even in the ring.

I don't wait for Ella to e-mail back. After dinner I video call her. It takes her six rings to answer, but when I finally see her face, my insides instantly relax.

"Ella!" I say.

"Hey, Skyler. I'm, um, well, I'm out right now," she says, all awkwardly. When she turns the camera to the other side of the booth at Three Scoops, our favorite ice-cream place, I see why.

"Oh, hey, Alex." I wave. Holy cow, are they on a date? I don't see anyone else in the background.

"Hi, Skyler." He waves before Ella turns the camera back to herself.

"I better let you go," I say. "Call me when you get a chance?"

"Yeah, of course," she says.

We say good-bye, and I don't even wait for her to hang up before I end the call.

I'm in *Italy,* and Ella is off having more fun than I am.

The way I see it, I have two choices.

One, I quit. Which Mom would NOT be happy about.

Or two, I finish these darn posts and use my last three (oops, now four thanks to Zara) to do something amazing. I'm in Venice, and I can pick whatever I want to write about. But I can't get there until I catch up on my assignments.

I consider flipping a coin or drawing straws with myself, but Logan is right. I need to figure it out and make a decision.

EIGHTEEN

Dear Ella,

I'm betting you had a great time with Alex yesterday. I hope you'll tell me all about it when you can.

It's not going so great here, but I'm determined to change that. I'm behind on my blog posts, so I plan to get everything written today.

Enough about that. Wait until you hear about Daniela and Patrizio.

The minute I get into the office on Thursday, I start on "A Glassmaker's Tale" and "Patrizio's

Story," fine-tuning until I get them just right. It is not easy to write when you feel stuck. But I make myself sit down in the chair and get the job done. When I take short breaks, I work on my e-mail to Ella, filling her in on everything here and all the cool inside scoops.

By lunchtime I've added the final touches to my posts, and I e-mail them to Marissa.

I'm feeling pretty good . . . until I run into Zara in the hallway. I'm not letting her off the hook with this one.

"You did it again," I say.

She's leaning against the wall doing something on her phone.

"Did what, Skyler?" asks Zara.

"You undermined me," I say, pulling out one of my fanciest words.

"I'm guessing this is about the post?" she says.

"It's about all of it, Zara," I say. "It's about teaching me the wrong words during my Italian lessons and making me break the rules by following Marissa and Logan and using my idea to scoop me on a post. All of it."

Zara tilts her head. "Come on, Skyler. We both know it was my idea."

"But I asked you if I could use it," I say.

"Did I say yes?" she asks.

I pause to think about what she's saying. "Well, not technically, but you didn't say I couldn't," I answer.

"So I used *my* idea and *my* title for a post that you tried to take credit for, and you're mad at *me*?" she says.

She's not backing down, but neither am I. "You made me think I could use it. Stop playing games with me." Oh my goodness, this girl is getting on my last nerve. MY. LAST. NERVE. "What's with you doing a total one-eighty?" I ask. "I thought maybe we could actually be friends after the other day."

"You don't understand," she says softly. "I need this internship. It's the only way my parents will let me stay here."

I give myself exactly one second to sympathize with her. "It doesn't make it okay to not play fair."

She takes a deep breath and lets it out slowly, looking at me the whole time. "I'm sorry. I should have told you I was planning to use it," she says. "But I'm not sorry I did it."

If that's how she's going to be, I'm certainly not going to tell her it's all right.

"Well, good luck to you," I say. "I hope you can live with the fact that you cheated to get there."

I'm so done with this conversation. I walk past her and head to Marissa's office.

"Hey, Skyler," says Marissa. "I'm just reading over your posts."

I'm not sure if that should make me happy or nervous, and right now I've got a whole jumble of emotions going on inside anyway.

"I worked really hard on them," I say.

"Why don't you have a seat, and I'll finish them up," she says, motioning to the chair in front of her desk.

I take out my phone to check for a message from Ella, but it's still pretty early in the States, so I'm not surprised that there's nothing. Her date must have gone really well, which makes me happy for her and sort of jealous at the same time. Even more wacky emotions dance inside me.

Marissa jots down notes as she reads, and every once in a while she leans in to the computer screen. Her expression doesn't change at all, so I can't get a hint at what she's thinking. All I can tell is that she has a lot of notes for me. A lot.

I take a few deep breaths, figuring this can't be good, but at the same time trying to convince myself that if she's still reading, that's a good sign.

When she's finished, she leans back in her chair and takes her own deep breath. I squeeze my hands together and sit very, very still.

Marissa picks up her notepad, comes around to the front of the desk, and sits in the chair beside me. "Skyler, I need you to be honest with me. Are you enjoying this internship?"

I'm ready to answer with an enthusiastic yes, but my brain tells me to stop and think. "Sort of?" is all I can muster, and judging by Marissa's expression, I know it wasn't the right answer.

"I'm afraid we're looking for more than sort of," Marissa replies.

"Were the posts that bad?" I ask. "I really did work hard on them."

"We can work on the writing," says Marissa. "There are definitely some things I can teach you that will make it more engaging to your audience, but your grammar, your spelling, and your sentence flow are all really good."

I give myself a second to take in the compliments.

"I can even see that you're making an effort to make your word choices more dynamic and that you're reaching outside your comfort zone," she says.

Hmm, more compliments. The middle of the compliment sandwich is for sure going to be a whopper.

"I am trying," I say.

"I'm very proud of you for that," she says.

"So what is it?" I ask. "Why don't you look happy?"

Marissa smiles a half smile. "It feels like you got them done just to get them done. What I'm saying is that the issue isn't your writing as much as your motivation," she says. "To be completely honest, the most motivated I've seen you is when you wrote that fake post to trick Zara. And that's just not what I'm looking for."

I lower my gaze and pick at fuzz on my shorts. "I understand."

"These last two posts, for example . . . I can tell there's an amazing story to be told, but there's no excitement or passion when I read between the lines," says Marissa. "It's just a retelling of a story you heard. There's no hint of who you are as a writer in those posts. Does that make sense?"

I nod.

"These posts are supposed to be about *your* view of Italy as an outsider. Your perspective on what you see and hear and experience. And I'm more than willing to guide you and be your mentor if writing excites you." Marissa puts her notepad on the desk and leans down on her knees. "What do you think about all this?"

I take a minute to figure out an answer. "I like writing," I say. "I mean, I didn't realize I was even any good at it until I got here. It makes me happy that I'm creating something, you know?"

Marissa smiles, which I take as a good sign. "That's what I was hoping you'd say."

I relax a little in the chair. "So what now?"

"How about focusing on the 'Only in Venice' theme for the time being?" says Marissa. "Is there anything you want to do here that you haven't done yet?" she asks.

I instantly know my answer. "I want to ride a gondola," I say. "I know, it's a totally touristy thing to do, but I haven't had a chance, and how can I spend a summer in Venice and *not* ride a gondola?"

"I completely agree," says Marissa. "Why don't you go have lunch, and we'll meet up in thirty minutes to head into the city."

I smile.

"And remember, I'm not looking for a list of facts. I've ridden a gondola before. I want to experience it through your eyes this time."

"Got it," I say. I stand up to leave, and a sense of relief washes over me. "Thank you, Marissa."

"You can thank me by giving all you have to your next post," she says.

And that's exactly what I plan on doing.

I literally run to my mom's office, almost toppling over a stack of pasta boxes on my way. "Sorry," I say to anyone who might have witnessed my less-than-graceful running.

Mom is on her phone, but she smiles when she sees me and holds up her pointer finger to let me know she's almost done.

When she hangs up the phone, she comes around the desk to give me a hug.

"Hey, sweetie. To what do I owe this midday visit?" she asks.

I didn't have much time to rethink what I'm about to do, which is why I ran here—so I couldn't talk myself out of it.

"I know you're busy," I say, "but Marissa is

taking me on a gondola ride in thirty minutes for a post and it's kind of an important post and it's also, you know, a gondola, and I was thinking that if I'm going to go on my first-ever gondola ride that it should be with you." I spit it all out at once so I can't chicken out. She could say yes, I remind myself.

But when she lets out a sigh and looks down at her shoes, I know what's coming next.

"I would love to," says Mom.

"But," I add for her.

She gestures to her desk and the stacks of folders in the to-do box.

I nod. "It's okay. I figured it was a long shot." I'm usually pretty good about staying composed, but right now the tears are not having it. I need to get out of here before I get upset and then Mom gets upset and I miss my chance to eat before going on my first-ever gondola ride without her.

I turn and wave over my shoulder. "See you later."

"Skyler," she calls. But I'm far enough away that I can pretend I can't hear her.

NINETEEN

When I get to Marissa's office a half hour later, I quickly realize it won't be just the two of us on this little jaunt. Zara is sitting in front of Marissa's desk saying how excited she is for this. Great.

"Hey," I say when there's a break in their conversation.

"Skyler," says Marissa. "I hope you don't mind that I invited the rest of the crew."

The *rest* of the crew? That means—

"You ready for this?" asks Logan as he walks up next to me.

I push my lips together to hide the enormous smile that's about to take over my face. It's ridiculous how the sound of his voice instantly puts me in a better mood.

"Can't wait," I say.

"Great," says Marissa. "We're just waiting for one more, then."

I take a mental count of who's here. Marissa. Zara. Me. Logan. "Who's one more?" I ask.

I get my answer when Gino pops his head in the doorway. "That would be me," he says.

This excursion is getting better and better. "Awesome," I say. "Let's do this."

We take the train into Venice and make our way to one of the ports where you can get a ride down the Grand Canal.

"Hey, when are we doing that Italian lesson?" asks Gino as we walk.

"I really appreciate you offering to help me," I say, "but I'm taking these posts one at a time right now. I think I kind of have to prove myself with this one first."

"Ah, gotcha," says Gino. "Well then, let's get you on that gondola."

Zara is clearly listening, but she doesn't say a word. Not in any of the million languages she speaks.

"Sounds like a plan," says Logan, apparently catching the end of our conversation. The five of us walk out from under the awning labeled SERVIZIO GONDOLE and walk down the stairs. The gondolier helps Zara in first, and I follow.

But here's the problem. There are two seats at each end facing each other and pillows on each side of the boat. We all look back and forth at one another, trying to figure out where everyone is going to sit. Where everyone wants to sit.

"Si siede, per favore," says the gondolier, in his red-and-white-striped shirt and wide-rimmed hat. He motions for us to sit as he helps Logan and Gino into the boat.

I go to the right, even though it means I'll be facing backward. I try not to worry about who's going to sit next to me, because at least I know Zara won't choose to. But before I even sit down, I see Logan rush to the seat beside me. Yeah, that works.

Zara doesn't look too disappointed. She's sitting next to Gino, who also seems quite happy with the seat selection. Marissa gives us all a look from her seat on the side, just in case we think she doesn't know what's going on.

It's like a parade of gondolas, one after another down the canal. Every once in a while a gondolier kicks off the side of the canal to help steer the boat. We pass under endless bridges as tourists cross from one side to the other. We pass motorboats, big and small, buildings of all different colors, and uniquely shaped windows—the arched ones are my favorite. Each gondolier wears a striped shirt—most are red and white, but some are blue and white—and black pants. I figure they're all about the same no matter what boat you get on, until one of them starts singing.

I lean over to Logan. "Hey, does our guy do that?"

"Maybe?" says Logan.

Gino gets up and moves to a seat near me. "Most of them do," he says. "But it's extra."

Well, apparently Zara is having none of this new seating arrangement because she cuddles right up next to Gino. But the gondolier is also having none of it and shoos both of them back to their seats in front of him, which I'm guessing is a balance thing. But when Gino goes back, he hands the gondolier something, which our guide quickly shoves in his pocket.

"What are you doing?" I whisper-shout across the boat, which, okay, is only a few feet.

Gino just smiles as the gondolier starts to sing.

Our gondolier is *amazing*. He sings in Italian, so I don't understand the song, but it's beautiful. I feel like I'm at an opera or something. He keeps right on singing and ducks his head as we pass under another bridge.

But I'm snapped out of my moment when I feel droplets on my face. "Oh man, is it raining?"

Zara laughs, and the guys have *uh-oh* looks on their faces. Marissa is totally engrossed in the singing gondolier and is paying no attention to us.

"What?" I ask.

I get my answer when Zara reaches her fingers in the water and sneakily splashes me with only a sprinkle of water. She stares at me with her trademark smirk. I hate that smirk.

"Cut it out, Zara." I wipe the water off the side of my face. The moment feels weirdly similar to the beginning of my summer back home. And not in a good way. But that's a whole other story.

Zara leans a little to her left again. Our gondolier is so into his singing, he doesn't seem to notice, but I'm pretty sure he wouldn't appreciate us tipping his boat over. I hear these things are handmade and cost as much as a car.

I try again. "I can't believe you'd stick your fancy little fingers in that water. Eww," I say, trying to appeal to her prissy ways.

It kind of works—she does a scan of the canal and sits back in her seat, wiping her hands on her shorts. "So are you just going to stay mad at me forever? I'm trying to say I'm sorry."

"By splashing me with lagoon water?"

"Do you even know how to have fun, Skyler?" asks Zara.

I can tell my eyes are totally bugging out right now. Marissa's focus has shifted to us, but she seems to be letting the situation play out. And in this moment, I don't care who hears what I'm about to say.

"Seriously?" I say loudly. "We're in this beautiful city, on a freaking gondola ride, with incredibly cute boys sitting next to us, and you're asking if I know how to have fun because I don't want to fall out of a boat into the canal?"

Logan bumps my shoulder with his, and Gino sits up straighter with his chest out like he's just been crowned king. Whoops. I definitely did not mean to admit the cute boys part.

But I'm stuck in this boat, and there is literally nowhere to go to escape the embarrassment.

"Let's get some pictures," Marissa says, totally changing the subject. "You'll want to remember this ride." Her phone is out and ready.

Yeah, great. Let's preserve this moment for all of history.

She points her phone at Zara and Gino first, pressing things on her screen and moving the phone closer and then farther away from her.

"It's not straight, Mom," says Gino. He reaches out and adjusts her phone.

I really wish Mom were here. Her pictures always turn out a little crooked, which I love to tease her about, unless I straighten the camera for her just like Gino did.

Marissa snaps a picture and then turns to me and Logan.

"Okay, say 'Venice'!" she shouts. But I'm not giving her my *This is the best thing ever!* smile, and she knows it. "*Smile* and say 'Venice.'"

Logan puts his hand on top of mine and gives me the sweetest look that's ever been sent my way.

Well, that makes me smile. And lightens my mood a bit.

"Now crazy pictures!" Marissa laughs. "Let's see how much fun you're having."

Despite one fifth of my companions, this actually *might* be the best thing ever. Zara sits with her hands on her hips like a supermodel, and Gino is crossing his arms in that *I just scored a touchdown* sort of way. I wrap my fingers around Logan's hand to brace myself as we each stretch to our respective sides with our arms out wide. Marissa turns from one side of the boat to the other, taking crooked photos.

"Got it!" yells Marissa. "Now selfies!"

She's so right. A gondola selfie is an absolute must.

"I'll get this one," I say. I get my phone in selfie mode, turn slightly so everyone is in the photo, and stretch out my arm so our gondolier and the canals and bridges of Venice are in the background.

"Did it come out?" asks Logan. "You have to send it to me."

"It's perfect," I say. I turn to my nemesis to prove I most certainly do know how to have fun. "At least it will be perfect once I Photoshop Zara out of it."

Zara gives me her trademark look as our gondolier gets back to rowing and singing.

"I'm trying to say I'm sorry," I joke, repeating her halfhearted effort from earlier. Zara laughs. A real, honest laugh.

I turn the camera so it points at me and hold it as far away as I can. I want one pic of just me, on this amazing adventure. Proof that even if I'm still trying to figure out who I am, at least I know I'm someone who gets out there to see the world.

TWENTY

When I get back to the apartment, I grab my laptop and start typing. Even with that rocky part, the gondola ride ended up being one of my favorite things I've done so far, and it definitely fits the theme "Only in Venice." Although you can technically ride a gondola at the Venetian hotel in Las Vegas, nothing beats the real thing.

The words flow out of me, one after the other like my fingers can't type fast enough for what I want to say. There's voice and enthusiasm, and it's definitely told through my eyes. I go way over the word-count range, but I'm guessing Marissa will be okay with that.

I even do some research like she suggested and include facts about gondolas and their history, careful to balance it with my point of view. I add a few links to information on Venice so Marissa can see I'm taking the assignment seriously and readers can get more information if they want it.

Mom pops her head in my room. "Are you interested in going out for some gelato?" she asks.

"Is that a serious question?" I say. "That's like asking someone if they'd like the million dollars you're about to give them."

"I'll take that as a yes," says Mom with a chuckle. "Come on, let's go!"

In the back of my mind I wonder if this dessert outing is her feeling guilty about not going with me today.

"Mom, if you have work to do . . ." I trail off, giving her a chance to stop me.

"Absolutely not," she says. "We could use some girl time." She waits, and even though it's clear she's trying not to show it, I can tell she needs me to make this okay for her. To tell her I'm not mad and that I understand.

"Girl time sounds perfect," I say. "I mean, I've been surrounded by these adorable boys all day, and I'm not sure I can take much more of it."

Mom and I burst out laughing. It feels good to laugh with her. To let everything else go and have this moment with my mom.

"I just need a minute to finish up," I say.

Mom nods. "Whenever you're ready."

But I'm not taking a chance and giving her any time to get a work phone call or change her mind.

I want to add a couple more links with information on Venice, so I do a quick search and pop them into the post. I sit back and read through it.

It's good.

Really good.

I remember that my fifth-grade teacher used to ask us one question when we turned something in. Not *Is it finished?* or *Did you check it over?* or even *Is it the best it can be?* She simply asked, "Are you proud of your work?" If you could answer yes to that, it was all that mattered.

This time I ask myself, out loud, "Are you proud of your work, Skyler?"

And I smile. Because I am.

* * *

The next morning I go right to Marissa's office. She's typing on her laptop, so I do a quiet knock on the open door.

"Hi, Skyler," she says with a pep in her voice.

"Good morning. I'm sorry to bother you first thing, but I was excited to see what you thought of the post," I say. I sit down in the chair in front of her desk.

"And I was very excited to read it," she says. "It's your best yet. I'm proud of you."

I was already proud of myself, but hearing her say that totally makes my day. I can't wait to tell Mom.

"Really good work, Skyler. I knew you had it in you to be a great writer," says Marissa.

She might have known, but I certainly didn't. This feels like a big moment for me. One of those accomplishments that convince you that you can do anything you dream of.

"I just have to check your links and then it's good to go," she says. "I've already got it set to post this afternoon."

I bounce in the chair. I have to call Dad and tell him to watch for it.

"Okay, I'll let you get back to work." I stand up and am almost out the door when I hear her tone change.

"Well, this isn't . . . ," she says to herself, leaning in toward the screen. She clicks a few times on the mouse. "Oh no, this one too."

I don't know if she's still working on my post or if she's moved on to something else. Should I slowly sneak away or stay and ask?

Click.

Click.

Click.

As the look on her face turns into an almost-scowl, with her eyebrows furrowed and eyes intense, I decide to get out of here, just in case. But three steps into my escape, she snaps out of her hyperfocused mode and calls to me.

"Hold on, Skyler." She's still looking at the screen, and clicking. Oh man, the clicking.

"Is something wrong?" I ask.

She leans back in her chair and gently pushes her laptop away from her. "I'm afraid so."

Uh-oh. What could I possibly have done to get this kind of response? I thought she loved it.

I'm so afraid of what she's going to say that I don't say a word. I don't even move from the spot I'm standing in. It's like my feet are superglued to the floor.

"We talked about fact-checking," she says.

I nod.

"Did you check these links?" she asks.

I'm about to answer *Yes, of course I did* when I realize that's not actually the case. Mom was waiting for me, and I grabbed the first few Venice links I could find.

"I reread the post, but no, I guess I didn't double-check all the links," I say. "Why?"

She lets out a breath with a heavy sigh and turns her laptop to face me. I still haven't moved, so I'm not close enough to see what's wrong. I take one slow step at a time until I understand why she's so disappointed.

Venice, Florida.

Venice Beach, California.

Venice Pizzeria . . . in Newfoundland, Canada.

I slowly let out all the air in my lungs, and it must be a good ten seconds before I remember to breathe again.

"I'm so sorry," I whisper.

Maybe I shouldn't care so much about an internship. About a temporary job that may or may not lead to some really amazing opportunities. But I do. And when it hits me how badly I screwed up, I can't stop the tears from trailing down my face one after another.

"Oh, Skyler." Marissa comes around the desk and gives me a big hug. I appreciate it and I need it, but it's not who I need it from. "You made a mistake, honey. It happens."

She guides me to sit and then takes a seat next to me. She's quiet while I let it all out, while I let go of all the fears and disappointments that are sitting beside all the happiness and excitement of the summer. I hadn't realized how much I'd been holding inside until I use up half her box of tissues.

"It's just a lot," I say with a sniffle. "This summer. Being here. The internship. Missing home. It's a lot."

Marissa gives me a compassionate smile, letting me know it's okay to feel this way. "You're overwhelmed," she says gently. "Which makes sense. It's obviously been an emotional summer for you, and you haven't had a chance to process it all."

I blow my nose again and toss the wadded-up tissue into the garbage can. "Yeah, but who am I to complain?" I say. "I get to spend my summer in *Italy*. I get how lucky I am."

Marissa leans forward. "It doesn't mean you aren't allowed to feel these things, Skyler."

I decide to get real with her. "I wanted that spot with the magazine so much," I say. "I wanted to win this thing so I could get away and do my own thing. But then I grew to love it."

"I believe you," says Marissa. "But after two error-filled posts and that unsupervised adventure . . ."

She doesn't need to finish her sentence. I simply nod.

"Maybe you should try something else for the rest of your time here. Something less intense," she suggests.

I'm not sure how long I sit in silence, but my thoughts are doing somersaults and my stomach feels like it's jumping on a trampoline inside my body. Here I go again, quitting yet another thing. Not that I have a choice.

"I guess if there's something else I can do, that would probably be best." I'd attempt to beg my mom to let me be done with all the interning, but we had a deal. Plus, I already know she won't budge.

"I can talk to accounting," Marissa offers. "I'm sure they'll be able to fit you in for another week or so. Maybe you'll find that it's something you really like."

Accounting. Stuck inside all day crunching numbers, instead of exploring the city and meeting new people.

"Okay," I say, defeated.

"I'll call Sofia, and you can head over there," she says. "Maybe some more . . . structured work will help you take your mind off of everything for a while."

I nod again, but all I can think is how royally I screwed things up.

TWENTY-ONE

Dear Ella,

I'm sitting at a cubicle pressing enter whenever the program on the computer in front of me prompts me to. Yeah, long story. I'm e-mailing you from my phone.

So I was kind of forced to quit the blogging internship, which I'm not very happy about. I actually found something I liked doing— something maybe I could be good at. I had a friend I got to hang out with (Logan, not Zara) and another potential friend willing to teach me Italian (Gino, not Zara). I had free rein of anywhere I wanted to go in Venice to write

about whatever I wanted. I had a shot at getting a
totally amazing role as a teen reporter where
I could travel all over Europe. And I messed it
all up.

 And now here I am in a cubicle.

 But instead of telling you about the inside of
a building in Italy, let me tell you more about the
outside . . . I finally got to go on a gondola, and
YES, it is every bit as awesome as you'd think.
(See attached blog post about the gondola ride.
Except don't click on the links.)

The accounting department was super excited to
have me for a couple weeks, but apparently, since
their mentor program is already filled, I'm going to
simply be a helper. Fun stuff.

 Enter.

 Enter.

 Enter.

 "Skyler?" Mom's voice comes from right behind
me. "I got your message. What are you doing in
accounting?"

 I spin my chair around a quarter of the way,
sure to watch for my next prompt on the screen.

"Marissa thought I should find something I'm more passionate about," I answer.

Enter.

Mom gives me a look. "What's going on, sweetie? Because if I had to pick something you were the absolute least passionate about, math and numbers would be on the list."

"I screwed up, Mom. She couldn't keep me in the writing internship, and this was all that was open," I answer.

Mom grabs a chair from the next cubicle, rolls it over, and sits down. "Talk to me."

So I do. I tell her how I totally screwed up by sending the wrong blog post, how I've been so, so behind in writing my posts, how Zara stole my idea and somehow got my post bumped down, how I included a link to a pizza place in Canada in the best thing I've ever written . . . all of it.

"So here I am, enjoying the rest of my summer in accounting," I say with as much sarcasm as I can manage.

Enter.

"Skyler, when I said I wanted you to do an internship, it was because I wanted you to learn something and be productive, not so you could press enter every thirty seconds." Mom takes my hand and wraps her fingers around it. "I can talk to Marissa."

"No," I say quickly. "It doesn't mean anything if my mother has to get my job back. Besides, she didn't force me to come here."

"You wanted to come to accounting?" she asks, surprised.

"I wanted to not be humiliated when my ineptitude surfaces again," I answer, spinning my chair back to face the screen.

"Ineptitude," Mom repeats. "Well, at least you've learned some fancy new words."

I laugh, but I still don't face her. "That might be one of my favorite things about writing—playing with words," I say. "I didn't know they could be so fun."

Especially when they're said with an Australian accent.

It hadn't even entered my mind before now, but giving up the writing internship also means giving up whatever time I had left with Logan.

Although it also means not having to deal with Zara, so . . . one for the plus column at least.

"I know you have work to do, Mom," I say. "Don't worry about me. I'll be fine."

Mom pats me on the hand and stands up. "We'll talk about this later, okay?"

I nod and keep staring at the computer. At least I have thirty seconds at a time to write to Ella.

Enter.

Mom gets up and walks away, but she runs into Sofia on her way out. I can't hear everything they're saying, but I catch enough to know they're talking about me. Of course they are.

I scoot my chair closer, making sure I can still press the enter key.

"I thought I was doing a good thing," I hear Mom say. "I wanted this trip to be a turning point for us. A chance at a new start."

"Have you not had a good time together?" asks Sofia.

"We've had a great time," says Mom. "I absolutely love spending so much time with my daughter."

Despite my current mood, I smile at her words.

"But it's not enough," says Mom. "You know she wanted me to go with her on her first-ever gondola ride? She literally ran to my office to ask me. I could see she was out of breath."

"That's good, no?" asks Sofia.

"It's amazing," says Mom. "Except . . . I was busy with work and had to say no."

I push myself up on the chair and peek over the cubicle wall.

"Oh dear." Sofia's face softens to a somber expression, and she touches Mom's arm. "You are showing her how a person goes after their dreams. It's important she sees you work hard."

Mom nods, but her shoulders slump.

"I thought so," she says. "It's why I insisted she do an internship. I thought it would give her a good work ethic. Help her figure out what she likes to do. But maybe she doesn't need that right now. Maybe what she needs is her mother."

I can't believe what I'm hearing. I also can't believe that my tear ducts *still* aren't dry, but apparently they're quite capable of raining down my cheeks all over again. I wipe the tears away with my fingers.

"Sofia, I apologize, but I don't think this placement is right for Skyler," says Mom. "Would you mind if I took her for the rest of the day?"

My eyes go wide. And when the click-clack of Mom's heels gets closer, I scoot my chair back to the desk and wipe my shirtsleeve under my eyes.

I can't see her, but I can feel Mom standing there. No footsteps walking away, no clink of her bracelets.

"Hey, Skyler?" she says, as if there's a question as to whether or not she should be here.

I turn toward her, and my expression must say volumes because she grabs my hand and pulls me up.

"What do you say we get out of here?" she asks. "I know it won't be your first gondola ride, but it'll be my first and I'd really like to share that with my daughter."

She doesn't wait for a response as we head out of the office and onto the street outside.

"Mom, this is totally unprofessional. I committed to this," I say halfheartedly.

"Skyler, you're thirteen years old, and you should be out there having a grand old time. Not stuck in a cubicle doing something you have absolutely no interest in."

I want to jump right up and wrap my arms around her and never, ever let go. But instead, I wait.

Mom puts both hands on my face and leans in close. "What do you want to do, Skyler?"

"I don't know," is what I try to squeeze out, but my lips are a little smooshed.

"I mean it," says Mom. "Right now, without anyone telling you what you *have* to do, what do you *want* to do?"

I peel her hands off my face and turn to the street. The little shops and cafés. The cobblestone. The awnings. The people. Patrizio.

I wave, and he waves back with a smile. I turn toward Mom.

"I want to write about this place," I say. "I want to preserve it all so that someday when I'm telling my kids about this amazing summer I had in Italy with my mom, I have all the details and the stories and the memories written down. I want to finish this."

Mom smiles so big, she could be the definition of the phrase "beaming with pride."

And then I get a dose of reality. "But I'm not doing the internship anymore, Mom. I quit."

She pulls me in for another hug. "Forget the internship. You're a writer, honey. The only way you quit is if you stop writing."

The only way you quit is if you stop writing.

I don't know if Marissa will ever be willing to read my work again, but that doesn't mean I can't write for myself.

TWENTY—TWO

Dear Ella,

Mom and I finally had a moment. I mean it—
we really did.

Get this, she took the rest of the day off on
Friday to spend with me. Whoa, right?

Anyway, Mom and I went on a gondola
ride (her first, my second). The gondolier
even let me pose with the paddle and
everything! (That's not a normal tourist thing,
but he gets a lot of business from Mom's
company, and she somehow talked him into
it. Go, Mom!)

It's not easy to become a gondolier—you

have to know the history and art of Venice,
study a foreign language, do an internship, and
take tests. Plus, the boats are expensive!

We spent the rest of the weekend doing
whatever we wanted. We even took one entire
day to walk around the city with no plans at all.
We had pizza for lunch *and* dinner—because
we can.

By the end of the day my feet were killing
me, but it was worth it.

Sunday night I start an e-mail to Ella. I'm about to
attach the cute photo Mom arranged today, but I'm
distracted when I get an idea. There *must* be an app
that lets you create your own postcards from photos and send them through the mail. I do a quick
search and find one easily, then I upload the photo
and type Ella a message. It even lets me pick a font
that looks like my own handwriting.

Hi, Ella!

I'm emailing you now about my gondola
rides! Major fun. (Imagine a salute emoji
here. lol)

I wanted to send you this photo (which just might be my favorite pic ever) and figured this would be way more fun than an e-mail attachment.

Mom even got me a super-cute striped shirt and a hat like the gondoliers wear.

It's so very Venice, don't you think?
xoxo Skyler

When I'm done, I put in Ella's address and let the app take care of sending her an actual snail-mail postcard. So cool! Then I force myself to focus on writing a story about my weekend. The problem is, despite having a head full of things to write about, I don't know where to begin.

I walk in the living room and plop down on the couch with my laptop. "I'm stuck," I say.

"I thought you wanted to write about the weekend," says Mom.

"Yeah, but I think Zara and Logan already wrote about a lot of that stuff," I say. "If I'm going to impress Marissa and convince her to take me back, I can't do the same story they've already done."

"Is that your plan? To try to earn back a spot?" she asks.

"I don't know yet," I say. "But if that's what I decide to do, I definitely have to have something different to show her."

Mom takes a book she's been reading from the coffee table and fiddles with the bookmark. "Well then, write about this weekend through your eyes. Zara can't possibly have written that."

She's right. Of course she's right. "I don't know, Mom. Maybe this is a silly idea."

I expect her to put the book down. To talk me out of my funk and convince me I should do this. That I have it in me and I shouldn't let anything stop me from reaching my goals.

But all she says is, "If you think so." Mom opens her book, sticks the bookmark between pages, and settles back in the chair.

Um . . . that's it?

Marissa pretty much fires me, Zara scoops me again and again, and Mom isn't jumping in to save the day? Or is this reverse psychology? Does she know I don't actually think it's a silly idea, so she's trying to get me to do it by acting like she doesn't care? *Do* I think it's a silly idea?

I've never been good at making my own decisions. I never really had to be because Ella always
decided what we'd do, what movies we'd watch,
and when we were in kindergarten, what we'd
build with our blocks and color with our crayons.
I don't think I want to be the one who makes decisions about my life. Am I even capable of doing
that?

So instead of opening my laptop and doing what
I probably, maybe, should be doing and writing a
blog post to prove Marissa made the wrong choice,
I change into my pajamas and finish my original
e-mail to Ella.

It turns into a very jumbled essay all about my
weekend and my woes, and it ends with *Wish you
were here to tell me what I should do.*

I put away my computer and turn on the lamp
next to my bed. This is the hard part of being away
because you want to be where you are, but you
also want to be where you were. I snuggle under
the covers and grab the book off my nightstand. I
study the cover and the title that seems to be reading my mind: *No Place Like Home.*

Yeah, that's for sure. Even if you're in Italy.

♪ ♪ ♪

Monday morning comes too fast. Mom is clanking dishes in the kitchen, and while I probably should get up and see what the plan is for the day, I stay exactly where I am.

Eventually she comes in to say good morning.

"Hey, sweetie." She pushes my hair to the side and kisses my forehead. "We didn't talk about what we'd do with you today. You can't stay in the apartment without supervision."

The part she's not saying is that if I had an internship to go to, we wouldn't have this problem. "I'm sorry, Mom. I can come to the office with you. I'll read and post some photos. I got a few messages from friends back home that I need to respond to. Plus, I bought a postcard to send to Travis. He says he's going cray cray seeing all the fun I'm having."

Mom and I laugh. Travis is the kind of kid who grows on you.

"So you've decided not to write?" she asks.

I shrug. "There's only a week of the internship left. What's the point?" For the first time I'm actually kind of glad we'll be heading home soon.

Mom sits down on the bed, and I scoot my legs over to make room. "There's something I need to talk to you about."

Uh-oh. That's not usually a sign of good news.

"You're making me do the accounting thing?" I ask with a forced chuckle, in case it's true.

"No, I said you didn't have to do that, and I meant it."

I wait.

"I think they're going to offer me the position, Skyler," says Mom. "How do you feel about staying for the year?"

I freeze in place. A week ago I would have been thrilled about staying. But now?

After a minute Mom breaks the silence. "That's a lot to drop on you first thing in the morning. Think about it and we'll talk over gelato later, okay?"

All I can do is nod. I mentally put "gelato" in the plus column for staying.

Mom pats me on the knee and leaves the room. I make myself get out of bed and get ready, and there's no way I can think about anything other than this huge decision in front of us. Or is it even something I get a say in? What if I want to go home and Mom wants to stay? After how far we've come, no way am I going to be apart from her.

"Hey, Mom?" I make my way to the table for breakfast.

"What is it, honey?" she asks.

"The school I'd be going to, are any of the other kids from the office going there too?" There's really only one name I want to hear.

"I think most of them," she answers. "Zara for sure." She stands still, probably waiting to see if that pushes me over the edge.

That is *so* not the name I wanted to hear.

TWENTY-THREE

Dear Ella,

I was so happy to get your e-mail this
morning! Honestly, I LOVE it here, but it's also
really hard being away. So thanks for sending
a little bit of home over to me.

It's day three of having nothing to do. I'm
sitting in a comfy chair in the break room,
reading my book. Well, trying to read my
book. I can't focus. I screwed everything up,
and there's nothing I can do about it.

And now it looks like we'll be staying here
for the year.

So I have no chance at the school-year

internship. A really awesome internship
where I would have gotten to continue to hop
around Venice and write about it. That means
I've also lost my shot at the teen reporter slot
for the magazine, which just might have been
the coolest thing ever.

I didn't care one bit about writing before I
got here, but now that I've had a taste of it, now
that I have all these things to say about this
incredible place and no one to say them to?
Now I want it.

If only I could take Italy home with me, you
know? Have all my friends back home, but also
canals and gondolas and history everywhere
you turn. And, most definitely, the food.

Thanks for listening, Ella.

Answers to your questions are below in mint
green (as always).

I try reading again but close the book since it's
impossible to concentrate.

I don't usually reread e-mails, but right now I
have all the time in the world and I want to hear
every word Ella has to say—again.

I read about all the fun she's having. Hanging

out with friends, going to the movies, bike rides with Alex—even cleaning out her closets sounds like more fun than what I'm doing. She's still doing her volunteer work at the animal shelter, even though it's not required for school anymore. I read her note again. And again.

Ella is a girl who knows what she wants. She's always known. She makes lists. She makes plans. She does each item one at a time until every single one is checked off.

I pull the Italy list she helped me write out of my bag. I was supposed to write three posts on learning Italian (I wrote one, which never got posted). I was supposed to write three posts on interesting facts about Venice (I wrote two, and Zara scooped the third one before I'd even written a word). I was supposed to write three posts on people and their stories (I wrote two, which didn't even make it past Marissa's desk).

UGH.

I am apparently not a person who completes lists. Usually anyway.

I go back to the e-mail to Ella, and it gets really long as I take every activity she lists and do my best to compare it to what I've been doing.

In a way, we've both been hanging out with
friends. Movies and bike rides for you, but walks
and gondola rides for me. You getting to be
around Alex, me getting to be around Logan. I
guess it's not all that different, yet super-duper
different at the same time.

When I'm finished writing, I close the lid of the
laptop and walk out onto the balcony. This could
be my home for the next year. And I'm not sure
whether to be super-happy about that, or super-
confused.

I go back inside and grab my book again, doing
my best to stay focused. But when Logan comes in
looking for a snack (what a surprise), I definitely
can't concentrate.

"Gidday, Skyler," he says.

"Hi, Logan."

I giggle, wondering what my friends would
think if I started throwing out a random "gidday"
here and there instead of "hello."

Logan smiles, but it's like he can't quite tell if
it's safe to talk about my lack of activities.

"Doing anything fun today?" I ask. Which probably doesn't help him decide what he should and shouldn't say.

"We're, um, well, we're going to Libreria Acqua Alta," he replies. When I give him a confused look, he elaborates. "It's supposed to be a really cool bookstore with a staircase of books and a gondola and everything."

I slip the bookmark inside the pages of my book and set it on my lap. "That sounds pretty cool. Have fun."

"Yeah, you too." Logan heads toward the door, then stops and turns back to me.

"What?" I ask. I imagine him walking over, sitting next to me, and saying that he can't possibly do any of this without me. My imaginary Australian accent isn't nearly as good as his real one, though.

"Skyler? Did you hear what I said?" Logan's voice brings me back to reality, but oh my goodness, he's actually walking toward me. He sits down next to me.

No way. Did I just use the Force to make that happen?

"No, sorry," I respond. "What did you say?"

He smiles, which instantly makes my stomach flutter. "I said you could probably come with us. I bet Marissa would let you if you asked."

The fact that he wants me to go makes me feel better, but as my dad would say, I made my bed and now I have to lie in it. "Thanks for thinking of me, but I don't think that's such a good idea."

"Okay," he says, getting up. "Have a good one."

When he leaves, I raid the cupboards, figuring if he's in here all the time, there must be some good stuff. But there are only a few bags of crackers left and a whole bunch of coffee. So that doesn't take up much of my day at all.

I walk down the hall and pop into Mom's office. "Hey, Mom."

"Oh, hi, honey. How's it going?" she asks.

I consider my answer for a minute. "Great. Yeah. My book is pretty good, and I chatted with Logan for a bit." I do my best to cover so she doesn't see how insanely bored I am.

"I wish I didn't have so much work to do, but I'm swamped," she says, motioning to the stack of folders on her desk, her open laptop, and . . . Is that an empty cup of coffee?

"Can I get you some coffee?" I ask.

Mom glances at her cup. "Oh, that would be nice. You don't mind?"

Ooh, this is perfect. I bet I can convince her to let me go out for a fresh cup. "Not at all. I could use some fresh air," I say.

Mom's eyebrows arch down. "There's coffee in the break room, sweetie."

Yeah, no way am I losing this chance to get out of here. "Mom. You're in Italy. You should not be getting your coffee from the break room," I say. "I'll run across the street to Patrizio's."

"Skyler." That's all she says. Like I'm supposed to know what she's thinking by the way she says my name.

Okay, I know.

"Mom, it's right across the street. I could really use a little walk," I say.

Mom sighs. "Okay." She stands up and hands me some money. "Take twenty minutes and get yourself a treat too."

That one gets a big smile from me.

I take really, really slow steps across the street from the office to the café. I'm hoping to catch Patrizio so I have someone to chat with, but I'm told he took the day off. I guess you shouldn't be expected to work full-time in your eighties.

I get a pastry and some water for myself, figuring I better wait on Mom's coffee so it won't be cold when I get it to her. If she's giving me twenty minutes, there's no way I'm going back there any sooner.

I take out my journal and read through the notes I took the last time I sat here at this table with Patrizio and Logan. There's so much here, I didn't know how to condense it into one short post. I thought I did the best I could, but Marissa is probably right that it was missing something.

I check my notes more closely. Maybe there's information I should have used instead. I could have retold just one of the stories, instead of trying to cram in everything he told us. But how does a journalist pick what to highlight, what to leave out, and which details absolutely need to be told? Patrizio's story would change depending on what I decided to put in there, and how am I qualified to determine which parts of his life story are the most interesting?

For just a moment I consider trying to rewrite the post, but then what would I even do with it? I close my notebook and just sit. It's already a scorcher of a day, but people are walking up and down the street like usual.

Like usual.

This will be my new usual. I won't just be visiting Italy, I'll be *living* in Italy. Temporarily of course, but still. Or what if it's not temporary? What if Mom loves it so much here and they're so happy with her work that we stay here? The idea has never even entered my mind before.

I can wait out the rest of this summer trip— bored to death—but I can't wait out a whole school year until I go home. I can't wait out forever. I have to find something to keep me busy. Something that's mine.

TWENTY-FOUR

Ella!

It's all I send, and I'm desperately hoping it's not too early for her to get it and respond. I waited until three o'clock to send it, figuring she'd maybe be up by nine.

She hasn't been able to keep up with all my e-mails, and to be honest, I'm not one hundred percent sure where they are on her priority list. But I'm not giving up, so if the mammoth e-mail I sent yesterday is too much, I can send her a quick text.

While I wait, I think about the fact that at least I'll have something fun to do later. Mom and I have plans for a walk and dinner (and, of course, dessert)—her idea.

Hey, Skyler! Everything okay?

Yes. And no. Sent you a LONG e-mail, but basically I'm confused.

When Ella says she hasn't had a chance to read the e-mail, I launch into an update and wait to hear what she has to say. Because while Ella never would have quit an internship (and there is a one million percent chance she would have gotten that internship), I'm guessing she won't be surprised that I'm still second-guessing my decision.

Maybe writing isn't for you? But you seemed so excited about it, she texts back.

There's too much to say, and to be honest, I really need to see a friendly face right now.

Video chat?

The incoming request to chat pops up immediately, and even though it's one tiny moment in my day, it makes me smile.

"Okay, tell me what's really going on," says Ella.

But I have to stop and think, because I still don't know how I feel about all this.

"I *was* excited about the internship," I say. "I thought I was maybe even a little bit good at it."

"What does your mentor think?" asks Ella.

"She had already said she didn't think I was

passionate about it," I say. "That my writing was good but was missing the motivation. And then I wrote this post that she loved, but I still managed to screw it up. The bottom line is that she needs someone committed to it, and I'm not sure I am."

Ella pauses. "Well, if it's just for part of your summer, how committed do you need to be?"

"Right. Maybe I didn't put enough effort into it because subconsciously I figured it wasn't a long-term thing. But . . ."

Ella stares at me through the phone, waiting. "But what?" she finally asks.

"Oh, right . . . you haven't read my last e-mail yet," I say.

She takes a deep breath and slouches in her chair. "You're staying, aren't you."

It's a statement, not a question, because she already knows the answer from my lack of response.

"Mom's pretty sure she's going to be offered a longer contract," I say. "Ella, I can't—"

But this time she cuts me off and finishes the sentence for me.

"You can't be away from your mom for a year," she says. "You're getting to spend so much time together, and you two have done so many cool things over there."

My heart swells but aches at the same time, and there is not a chance of stopping the tears that are now trailing down my cheeks.

"I get it," says Ella.

Maybe that's the hardest part of all of this, that the people who get it are a million miles away right now.

As I try to think of something to say, I notice a bowl of hard candy on the desk behind her. "Hey, what happened to all your Starbursts?" I ask. They've always been her go-to stress reliever.

"I figured out that Jolly Ranchers last longer and don't get stuck in my teeth," she says with a chuckle. "Although Mom thinks I should switch to cheese sticks or yogurt-covered pretzels."

I smile, thinking about all the little things we know about each other. "She's probably right," I say.

"Well, I don't need them for the anxiety so much anymore," she says. "Mom got me a meditation app, and I'm practicing breathing techniques. Smart, right?"

"Definitely." Hearing about the little changes in her life makes me want to be there. "I'm so homesick, Ella," I say. "I miss you guys. Even Travis." I pull myself together and get closer to the screen. "Don't you dare tell him I said that. It'll go straight to his head."

We both laugh, knowing full well that Travis's exact response would be that I'm cray cray for missing home when I get to live in Italy.

"He *has* mentioned how lonely it is without you next door," says Ella.

Yeah, neighbors are the best. I haven't even met the other people in our building here.

While I could sit and mope about this for the rest of the day, Ella has a different plan.

"Okay, so it looks like you're going to be living in Italy," she says. "Skyler, that is incredibly cool and I'm super jealous, so don't you dare spend the entire year wishing you were somewhere else."

She's right. She's always right. Still my voice of reason.

"I don't know what to do, Ella," I say.

"What do you want to do?" she asks. "I mean, we already made a list of things for your blog posts, but forget that. What's one thing you absolutely want to do while you're there?"

I think about what she's saying and the fact that

she's only asking me to make a list with one thing
on it. One thing. *Come on, Skyler, you can think of
one thing you want to do while you're in Italy.*

"I should probably still learn some Italian," I
say. "Although I do know how to say 'pigeon.' And
'turnip greens.'"

Ella giggles. "That's great. But is it that you
should learn some Italian, or do you *want* to learn
some Italian?"

Friends have a way of making everything clearer
for you. They can see outside the fog you're in and
guide you through it. As soon as she asks the question, I have my answer.

"I *want* to learn Italian," I say.

"Perfect," says Ella. "You're starting a new Italy
list. Number one, learn Italian."

I smile at her. "You're not going to make me
write anything else on the list?"

"Nope," she says. "This is a Skyler list. See, an
Ella list would be long and detailed, but a Skyler
list is one thing at a time."

One thing at a time. That makes so much more
sense to me.

"I need to see what's coming next," says Ella.
"I need a plan. But you're the free spirit, Skyler.

You just need to take the first adventure and see where it leads you. I can't believe I'm saying this, but that's perfectly okay. For you." She giggles again, because "seeing where it leads you" is my thing for sure.

I grab my notebook and flip to a new page.

"Skyler's Italy List," I say as I write it at the top of the paper. "You're totally right, Ella. I don't need my whole year planned out, I just need to get started on it."

I'm about to close the notebook, but I stop.

"Maybe there's one other thing I want on the list," I say.

"What's that?" asks Ella.

I write it down and turn the paper to show her. *Stay connected.*

I look right into the little camera on my phone. "No matter how many e-mails I need to write, I'm going to tell you all about my year, and I want to hear all about yours." I say. "Deal?"

Ella smiles a true-friend kind of smile. "Major deal."

We both salute and say, "Major Deal."

"And, Skyler?"

"Yeah?"

"Stay connected to your mom too, okay?" she says. "I know it's not always easy, and maybe you can't see it yet, but I can."

There it is again, Ella guiding me through the fog.

"Thank you, friend." I give Ella a big phone hug, and as soon as we're disconnected, I pull up Gino's number.

I'm ready for my Italian lesson if you're still up for it, I text.

As if he'd been listening in on my conversation with Ella, he writes back, **Great! I'm free now. Want to get started?**

Yes, I text back. Because yes, yes I totally do.

It's only been an hour of Italian lessons with Gino, and I've already learned more than I did with Zara. I know how to say the basics like "hello" (*ciao*), "good-bye" (*arrivederci*), and the all-important "Where is the bathroom?" (*Dov'è il bagno?*), and we've discussed the similarities to Spanish, which helps me remember some of the vocabulary.

Mom also signed me up for an online program that I can do during her workday.

"Thank you so much, Gino," I say. But he gives me a look like I've done something wrong. "Oh, sorry, *grazie*."

That makes him smile, and he answers with *"Prego."* Which, for the record is *not* a spaghetti sauce; it means "you're welcome."

I still have at least a half hour before Mom is done working, but Gino has to get home. We plan to meet up again tomorrow, and I'm supposed to practice my Italian in the meantime. So as I walk back to the break room, I say *ciao* to literally every person I see in the hallways, and just for fun, I ask a few people where the bathroom is. Let's be clear, I have no idea what they say in return, but when they point, I head in that direction so at least they think they've helped.

I sit out on the balcony of the break room and pull my laptop from its sleeve. I consider playing a game or going on social media, but instead, I decide to start the Italian program. As I go to open it up, I catch a glimpse of my files—the ones that never did get posted to the company blog.

I stare at them.

Don't open them, Skyler. I try to convince myself

there's no use going backward, yet I still hover the cursor over the file for "A Cautionary Tale." The real one. The one I meant to send Marissa about my first Italian lesson with Zara. If you can call it that.

I double-click and open it.

It's one of those moments when you read something you wrote a while ago and since you're kind of removed from it, you've forgotten what you wrote.

And you know what? It's not so bad. I mean, it's actually pretty darn good. But as I read through the whole thing, I understand that Marissa is right. There's still something missing. An oomph. A different perspective. A clear motivation.

I think of the test questions we get at school. *Why did the author write this article?*

But that's the thing—right there. Why did I write this article? Because I was supposed to? That's why there's no motivation.

I needed to write this article to share my experience. To connect with readers. To put something out into the world that's all mine, through my eyes.

Against my better judgment, I study it and decide on a plan to fix it.

I compare that day to my lesson with Gino today. I mention words I've picked up while we've been here, like *caffè*—because when you spend as much time as I have in the break room, you learn the word for "coffee." I write about my emotions, like I do when I write to Ella. Because that's what this is missing: it's missing me and my voice. Only I can write this story . . . because it's *my* story.

Whatever it takes, I'm at least going to finish it.

TWENTY-FIVE

The next day I can barely wait to reread the post I worked on yesterday.

"What's going on with you?" asks Mom. "What happened to the bored look I've been getting all week?"

I smile and grab my bag. "I found some things to do," I say. "Gino is giving me Italian lessons, I'm going to start on that program you found for me, and I have some revising to do."

Mom looks pleased, which makes me happy. "That's great, honey," she says. "I'll try to finish up early today so we can go into Venice later. Sound good?"

I'd almost forgotten it's already Friday and

we'll have the whole weekend to soak up Venice. "Sounds great," I say. "Really, really great."

When we get to the office, I dive right in. I pull up each post I've written and decide what I can do to make them better by using Marissa's notes as a guide. I pick one to start with: "Patrizio's Story."

I can see it now. I understand what Marissa was saying and how I can revise it to make it more interesting. I need to do more than tell his story; I need to *show* the reader his story.

I spend the whole morning working on it, and then I set it aside to move on to "A Glassmaker's Tale." I grab some lunch, taking it out on the balcony as I hop to another post. When I finally stop and look at the clock, I have twenty minutes until I have to meet up with Gino. I haven't even seen Zara or Logan the last couple days, so I send a quick text to see what they've been up to.

Logan responds quickly with: **Sorry. Been all over.** Which makes me both a little jealous and sad at the same time. I miss hanging out with him. I might even miss Zara the tiniest bit.

We spend a few minutes texting back and forth,

and before I know it, it's time for my Italian lesson.

I'm about to close my laptop, but I stop. These stories are better now. And that's the thing—they're not just blog posts anymore, they're stories. Real stories.

They *could* just live on my laptop. Or maybe I'll open them up fifty years from now and it'll be enough for them to spark my memories of that amazing summer I spent in Italy with my mom.

But there's one more person I want to read them. If for no other reason than to say thank you for pushing me and showing me what it means to be passionate about something. Maybe it'll prove that I am a hard worker, and while I didn't step it up for the internship, I did learn something.

I open up a new e-mail, attach the files, and write a quick note to Marissa.

> Thought you might like to see these. Thank you for your notes and encouragement.
> Despite my lack of motivation originally, you made me see what was missing and you've made me a better writer.
> Skyler

I press send, and a wave of accomplishment makes me smile.

Mom and I are walking through Venice on Saturday before a tour we decided to go on. I've seen so much here already, but I want to know everything. I want to hear the little-known secrets that only the tour guides can tell you. I want to see the places we wouldn't know to look for on our own.

"I read your story," says Mom out of the blue.

"What do you mean?" I ask.

Mom leads me to a bench, and we sit down. "You left your laptop open on the coffee table last night when you fell asleep," she says. "I went to close it for you, but you had this story up about Patrizio."

"Yeah, I revised it and wanted to read it again," I say. "Sometimes it's better later, you know?"

Mom smiles. "It was fantastic, honey. I only meant to read one line, but I couldn't stop. I sat down and finished the entire thing. And then I wanted to read more."

"Really?" I ask. "Did you read anything else?"

"Yes, really," she says. "And no. I saw that you had other files open, but I didn't feel right reading them without your permission."

"But you *wanted* to read more?" I ask.

"Absolutely," answers Mom. "I've been inside working so much that I haven't had a chance to learn these things. To meet these people and get to know their history and their culture. But you have. You did such a wonderful job, Skyler."

I take a minute to think about everything she's saying. Mom isn't a writer, but she knows how to make something powerful and lasting by using the right words. So what she's saying means a lot.

"You can read them," I say. "I mean, I'd love it if you'd read the rest of them."

Mom takes my hand and gives it a squeeze. "I'd love to. I can see that you've worked really hard and that being a writer is something you enjoy."

Being a writer is something you enjoy.

It's weird that I need to hear other people tell me that before I believe it. "Thanks, Mom."

Mom's smile starts small, but it gets bigger and bigger until she looks like she's about to burst.

"There's something else," she says. "I'm hoping you'll think it's good news."

Which means it has the potential to go either way. Hmm. "What is it?" I ask.

"They offered me the position, Skyler," says Mom. "We're staying in Italy."

I let out a loud breath, trying to slow down the jumble of thoughts in my head right now. But I make a decision. To be happy.

"Mom, that's . . ." I squeeze my hands together and smile so hard, my cheeks hurt. "Are you serious? We get to *live* here?"

She nods excitedly, and within seconds, I'm tackle-hugging her. An entire year in this incredible place.

"Congratulations! You are totally amazing, Mom." I think of the conversation I overheard and how Mom working hard is showing me how to go after my own dreams. I want her to know that I see it. "You make me believe I can do anything, you know that?"

Mom's eyes instantly fill up with tears, and with one blink, they're released down her cheeks.

"I love you, Skyler," she says. "More than anything in the world."

And now I'm crying.

"I love you too, Mom," I say. "Even more than gelato."

We both giggle and wipe at our faces. Mom gives me a real mother-daughter hug, and I soak up every second of it.

But I get a notification on my phone, breaking up this moment. It's an e-mail from Marissa.

"I sent the files to Marissa yesterday," I say, punching the unlock code into my phone.

Mom leans over my shoulder. "What did she say?"

I scan through the e-mail. "She says they're really improved. Wow . . ."

"What?" asks Mom. "Don't keep me in suspense."

"And she loved them," I say. Inside, I'm super excited, but I also can't believe it. "She wants to know if I have anything else."

"Do you?" asks Mom.

"No. I sent her everything I had. Do you think she wants to use them?" I ask. "Should I write more just in case?"

Mom scoots back a little. "Do you want to write more?" she asks.

The funny thing is that I don't really have an answer. I loved making those stories better, but do

I want to put myself through that again if Marissa doesn't even want them? Maybe she was just asking to be nice.

"I don't know," I say. "I kind of like that I don't *have* to, you know? I think it was so fun because I was working on them for me."

Mom checks her watch and gets up from the bench. "That's the best kind of writing," she says. "Let's go on that tour and see what else we can learn about Venice." She holds out her hand and helps me off the bench.

I don't know if I'll be sending anything else to Marissa, but I have my notepad ready to write down what I learn today. I want to remember everything about this day.

I set my phone to camera mode. "Hey, Mom, selfie?"

She leans in like she's a pro, and we both smile for the camera.

TWENTY-SIX

On the way back from a seriously cool day trip to Verona on Sunday (where we got to see Romeo and Juliet locations, and Juliet's balcony!), I take out the postcard I bought for Dad. On the front there's a photo of the Verona Arena, which is a really cool Roman amphitheater that's still used. (They've fixed it up a bit.)

Dear Dad,

Don't worry, Mom and I haven't seen everything in Italy yet.

But you might want to hurry up and get over here. 😊

Miss you.
xoxo Skyler

I don't even know if it'll get to him before we go back to New York to pack, but picturing him walking to the mailbox, opening it up, and smiling is really the point. I'm kind of loving this postcard thing. It's like a message in a bottle that you send off to sea.

As soon as we walk in the door to our apartment, I get a text from Logan.

Meet up for pizza?

Even though I've been asked that a million times since I've been here, the answer is always yes.

I haven't seen Logan since Wednesday, and it dawns on me how much I'd miss him if I weren't staying. One for the plus column.

There's a little restaurant near our apartment, and since Mom can see us from the window, she lets me and Logan go on our own, as long as I promise to bring her back a slice—or two.

"Italian lessons, huh?" asks Logan after I fill him in on what's been going on.

Sì, I answer proudly. Since it means "yes" in both Spanish and Italian, it's super easy to remember. "And the tours my mom and I went on were amazing! I learned so much. Do you know why most of the bridges in ancient times didn't have steps on them?" I ask.

"No. Why?"

"Because so many people used to get around on horseback," I answer. Logan shakes his head. "You're like the guru of Venice now. What else?"

I take out my notebook to find one of the most interesting facts to share with him. I have a whole list. "You know the bell tower at St. Marks's Square?" I ask.

"Yeah," he answers. "Don't tell me it's haunted."

"No." I laugh, thinking of our haunted Venice tour. "It's one of the tallest bell towers in Italy. People say it's the best view of Venice from up there."

He leans forward on the table. I'm getting the hang of this "hook your reader" (or listener) thing. "Well, is it?"

"I don't know. We didn't have time to go up, but

it is definitely on my list now." I pull out my phone. "Seriously, though, you have to see some of these pictures from the tour." Logan scoots his chair next to mine, and I scroll through all my pictures, giving him whatever info I know about each place.

I pick up what's left of my pizza and savor the last couple bites.

"I'm glad you're having a good time," he says. "You were pretty miserable the last time I saw you."

"Yeah," I agree. "I was seriously bored. But once I decided to do something about it, I started having a pretty good time. I'm kind of kicking myself for losing out on the chance to share all of this. I think maybe I could have had a shot at really doing something great, writing-wise."

Logan doesn't take long to respond. "Looks like you're doing something pretty great to me."

"I know, I guess, but it would have been cool to do it officially," I say. "Especially since we're staying."

It doesn't dawn on me until the words leave my mouth that Logan didn't know yet.

"You're staying?" he says with a smile on his face.

I nod. "The whole year," I say.

It's quiet for a few moments—that comfortable kind of quiet you have with good friends.

"That's great news, Skyler," says Logan.

I'm pretty sure I could just sit and stare at him for the rest of the day, but a notice pops up on my screen, snapping me out of my thoughts. There's a picture of Ella, Alex, Travis, and a couple of our other friends from back home at Three Scoops.

Nothing better than ice cream with friends! Miss you!

Which gives me an idea. "I need a picture of us—with dessert," I say.

"Okay." Logan doesn't even ask why.

"We can stop back here afterward and get the slices of pizza for my mom," I say.

We head down the street just a little and study the display case, which is full of metal bins of gelato. It's never easy to choose a flavor.

Once we have it, I stand next to Logan, put my phone in selfie mode, and hold up my gelato—lavender this time. Yeah, lavender. Who knew?

"I'll take the picture," he says. "I have a longer arm."

He snaps it, and I send it off to Ella with the caption, **Totally agree! Miss you too!**

When the message comes back, I quickly tilt the screen so Logan can't see it.

THAT'S your crush?! OH. MY. AUSTRALIA.

Logan stands there, looking at me.

"What?" I ask.

"Too bad you didn't spend as much time writing posts as you did sending texts and e-mails and postcards to your friend Ella."

I have to admit, he's right. I definitely could have put more effort into the internship. Maybe I should just save my e-mails to Ella so Future Me can read about my epic summer.

Hmm.

"Wait a minute," I say. "Logan, you're a genius! I *do* have more to send Marissa!"

He leans away a little. "Hold on, what exactly are you talking about?" he asks.

"I'll explain everything, but I need my laptop. Will you help me?"

He doesn't have a clue what I'm asking of him, but I'm too excited to stand here and explain.

"Of course," he says, and I appreciate his friendship even more right now.

"Great! Let's go." Before I can think about what I'm doing, I give him an enormous hug.

TWENTY-SEVEN

Dear Ella,

Would it be okay if I share our e-mails? Turns
out I've been writing about my summer
through my eyes all along.

Logan and I set up at the kitchen table, and Mom
calls his parents to let them know he's here with
us. I finally explain my plan to Logan.

"You were totally right," I say. I give him a
moment to let that sink in. I know from watching
my parents that when one person says "You're
right," the other one wants a minute to enjoy it.
"I spent so much time writing to Ella about my

summer that I didn't have anything left to put into my blog posts. The e-mails to her are the ones that have the passion and motivation that Marissa was looking for all along."

I open my e-mail account and scroll down to the first one I sent off. Logan and I spend the next hour copying and pasting them into documents and adding the dates so I can keep them in order.

"The question is, are you going to leave these exactly as you wrote them so they're completely authentic, or do you plan on editing them?" asks Logan.

Hmm. On the one hand, authentic is the way to go. They would be real, and maybe kids would relate to them more knowing that they're not perfect. On the other hand, now that I'm sort of officially a writer, I don't know if I want my work out there with typos and grammar mistakes. Then there's the content. I'm pretty sure I complained about Zara in there a few times. And there is *for sure* a mention or two about the cute Australian boy. Although, if I'm really going for authentic, I might have to suck it up and leave that in.

"You're doing some serious thinking there," says Logan.

I don't even know how long I've been sitting here, but now both he and Mom are looking at me.

"Logan was just telling me what you guys are doing," she says.

Seriously? Was I that deep in thought that I didn't even hear them talking?

"I think it's very clever. That's my girl," says Mom.

Her smile means the world to me.

Once she goes off to do her own thing, Logan asks me again, "So are we editing?"

I give it one last thought before I answer. "A little bit," I say. "I do want it to be authentic, but there's no reason to have mistakes in there. And I think I might want to focus on other things than my fighting with Zara."

I laugh, because as much of a pain as she's been, she *has* kept me on my toes. She might have even taught me a few things about the real world.

"But I do mention *you*," I say.

"Oh?" His eyebrows go up and he smiles. Logan is not going to let me off the hook here.

"Listen, this is totally embarrassing to admit, but of course I'm going to mention the sweet Australian boy I'm working with." I rally up my courage and continue. "It's not every day that happens."

He laughs. "Well, it's possible I also wrote my mate Liam and told him about the nice American girl I'm working with."

I don't even bother trying to hide my huge smile. "You said that?" I ask.

"I did." He pauses, as if he's debating whether or not to tell me more. "I also said you were a whole lot of fun and made me want to go to work every day."

Whoa.

What I really want to do is call Ella so we can dissect this conversation word for word and talk for hours about exactly what he meant. But instead, I force myself to focus on the project.

"So, yeah, um . . . You're okay with me mentioning you, then?" I finally say.

"Definitely."

I turn the laptop so that both of us can see it. "How about if I read these to you and fix them up as I go, and you can look through my pictures for ones that go along with the e-mails."

It takes us a few hours, but all the parents are cool with it since not only is it summer, but we're actually doing work.

"I think that's it," says Logan after we've uploaded all the files and pictures. "All that's left is to send Marissa the link to it all. You ready?"

I take a deep breath and type in her e-mail address. "What should I say?"

"Keep it simple," he says. "She's the one who asked if you had anything else."

"That's true." I type what I want to say a few different ways and finally decide on the right words. "How does this sound?

'Hi, Marissa. It turns out I do have more to show you. I've been writing to my friend Ella since I've been here and didn't realize until today that I've been doing exactly what you asked at the start of all this. So here is my story of living in Italy this summer, through my eyes, as I would (and did) tell it to a friend. I hope you enjoy it.'"

Logan nods. "Perfect," he says. "Send it."

I put my pointer finger above the touch pad and do a dramatic tap to send it on its way.

TWENTY-EIGHT

When I go into the office on Monday, I head straight to the break room. Only three more days until Mom is done with her initial contract here, and then we get a little break. The plan is to go home to New York and get things packed up so we can rent out our house while we're here for the year. Dad already has renters and is taking care of all the paperwork.

It's kind of weird thinking of someone else living in our house and sleeping in my bed (we're renting it out as "furnished" so we don't have to worry about storing all the furniture somewhere). My job is to figure out what I absolutely have to have for the year, what I want to put in storage, and what things it's time to part with for good. Ella and my friends back home have already offered to help. I'm totally pushing for endless sleepovers to get it all done. Mom and Dad have a much bigger job with the rest of the move.

We're sort of staying where we are here, but we're moving into a bigger apartment in the same building. Since Dad will be working from home (or, I guess, our new home), he needs another room for an office. So before we leave Italy, Mom and I need to move our things to the new place. Logan and his parents have offered to help, which will make it much easier. It's not like we have all that much here with us, and our new place is furnished too, but it's always nice to have help to make it go faster.

On my way to my regular spot for the day, Marissa calls from her office. "Skyler, hold on a second." I stop and go in. She comes out from behind the desk. "Do you have a minute?"

I laugh. "I have more minutes than I know what to do with," I say. I should be nervous like I have been the other times I've waited for her feedback, but this time I'm not. I'm proud of what I sent her, and if all she has to say is that she wishes me well, so be it.

"Please, have a seat." I do as she asks as she closes the door and sits down in the seat next to me. It's much more casual than her usual behind-the-desk stance.

"I'm guessing you got my e-mail," I say. "I just thought maybe you'd like to see it. I mean, I kind of wanted to say thank you for helping me see what I needed to do."

Marissa smiles. It's not a forced *Oh boy, now I have to think of something nice to say about her writing* smile. It's genuine. It's happy.

"Thank you, Skyler," says Marissa. "I really appreciate that." She scoots her chair so she's facing me. "But I also wanted to tell you that I absolutely loved it." There's that smile again. I like that smile. "*Loved* it," she repeats.

"Really?" I ask. As much as I would have been okay with her not loving it, this is even better. Way better.

"Funny how you'd been doing your assignment all along," she says. "You were just sending it to a different audience."

"Yeah, it took me a while to realize that," I say.

"I can't offer you one of the internship spots," says Marissa. "It wouldn't be fair to Logan and Zara."

"I understand," I say. "I really wasn't trying to get the internship back. I just wanted to share my writing with you."

"I'm so glad you did. And while I can't give you the internship, I also can't let this get away from me without posting it. It's too good. It's exactly what I was looking for." She grabs her laptop from the desk, taps a few keys on the keyboard, and turns it to show me. "What do you think of this?"

I can't even believe what I'm seeing. There's a sort of logo on the side of the *Travel Adventures* blog with a girl walking across a stone bridge. The text above it says, *Dear Ella*.

"What is that?" I ask.

Marissa taps the keys again, and my first note to Ella shows on the screen. "I'd like to publish your letters as a weekly column," she reveals. "Every Tuesday people will get another little peek into your adventures here."

I can't believe it. It's perfect. It's my story, on the screen, and people will be reading it and maybe, *maybe*, even looking forward to reading the next one each week.

Marissa chuckles. "I'm not sure if I should take your silence as a yes or an absolutely not."

"Yes," I spit out. "It's a yes for sure."

"Great. I'd like to put the first one up right away. Then you can settle into your new school routine and don't have to worry about handing in any more assignments. But you'll still get credit for writing for the company. Might look good on your résumé someday."

Wow. Just wow.

"I do need one more thing from you," says Marissa. "As it stands now, your series of letters just sort of ends. I'd like another post to wrap it up. Do you think you can write Ella one more letter?"

I nod. My words are gone. Gone.

"Whatever you want," she says. "Go do something on your list and send it to Ella. We want to keep it authentic. But then send it to me."

I nod again.

"I can see you're a little overwhelmed," she says. "I'll have a chat with your mom and make sure all of this is okay."

When she gets up and walks to the door, I follow

her lead. I somehow manage to get out a couple words. "Thank you," I say.

"Thank *you*," says Marissa. "Nice job, Skyler."

I almost can't believe it, but I've finally learned to give myself some credit and I know I earned that column.

"Oh, and because of this, I might still be able to submit your name for that teen reporter role with the magazine," she says. "I know how much you wanted that."

I take a deep breath and let it out slowly. Not because I'm disappointed, but because I'm relieved.

"Thank you," I say, "but I think I'd like to withdraw from consideration."

"Really? Why?" she asks.

I think of running through the streets of Venice with my mom and dad, and I imagine all the things we could do together on the weekends.

"I thought I needed to make my own adventures and that the teen reporter job was the only way to make it happen," I say. "But it turns out this is exactly where I want to be."

I leave the office walking on air. And if it's

possible, after hopping from one thing to the next
all this time, I might have finally found something
I'm good at and somewhere that inspires me to be
even better. But most of all, a bunch of someones
who believe in me.

TWENTY—NINE

When Mom hears the news about my column, she decides to finish her contract early. Let me say that again so I believe it myself: My mom told her work that she needed off Tuesday and Wednesday and would be back to finish up everything on Thursday instead. For me. Because apparently she can do that.

She says she has a surprise for me, and all she tells me is that we're heading out of Venice for a couple days and that I should pack a few things. When we get on the train, I still have no idea where we're going and I'm loving it.

I did bring a book, but Mom and I end up talking and spend an hour catching each other up on things. Mom's job is actually pretty interesting. I ask question after question as she tells me about the project and what she'll be doing while we're here for the year.

But then it's quiet, and as we sit there, Mom just watches me. She's got that "mom look" on her face, where mothers seem to be thinking something and feeling something that only a parent can understand.

"What?" I finally ask.

Mom reaches over and grabs my hand. "I was sitting here thinking that I've always worked hard because I thought it was what was best for our family," she says. "But in the process I've missed so many things."

I'm not sure what to say, so I stay quiet.

"Coming here, with you, was supposed to be my grand gesture that I'd changed that," she says. "But I haven't. Not yet."

"You've been focused on work, Mom," I say. "I get it. It's important to you. I guess this trip has made me see how much your job means to you."

Mom gives me another mom look. This time it's the *How did I get such a wonderful daughter?* look.

"*You* mean more," she says. "I want you to know that. Work is something we do in life, and yes, I love my job, but being a mom . . . being *your* mom . . . that's the most important job I'll ever have."

I swallow. I take a deep breath. I even successfully manage to hold back the tears. It's a moment I won't ever forget, because instead of telling me she has to rush back to work after this trip, instead of patting me quickly on the back and pulling out her laptop, she wraps her arms around me. Tight.

"Skyler, we're here," says Mom, waking me up with a nudge.

I scan my surroundings and remember we're still on the train. "Where?"

"Parma," she says.

I should have a better idea of where everything is in Italy, but I still have a lot to learn. I ask my phone, "Where is Parma?" and a map appears on the screen. We're southwest of Venice in the center of the country, not near the water that we've now gotten used to.

Time for my next question. It's of course intended for my mom, but I ask my phone again. "Why are we in Parma?"

Mom laughs. "You'll see."

She makes a call, and we meet a driver outside the train station. Within minutes, we're at our destination—although I'm still not sure what it is. Until we go inside.

"We're taking cooking classes," says Mom with a huge smile on her face. "Fun, right?"

I can't believe I never thought of it before. "Mom, that is seriously an awesome idea."

She wraps an arm around me and gives me a squeeze. "I figured we couldn't leave Italy without knowing how to cook some of these things back home, right?"

"Right," I answer. Even though we'll be here for a year, the idea of being able to cook for my friends while we're home next week makes me happy. "What are we making?"

"Let's find out," says Mom.

We get checked in, and the day is a whirlwind from there. The kitchen is amazing. State-of-the-art equipment, our own aprons and chef hats, seriously talented chefs, and insanely delicious smells.

First we learn to make fresh pasta. Flour, eggs, and a pinch of salt. That's it. We mix it and flatten it and send it through the pasta machine. We lay it out to dry, and I cannot wait to try it. Next we make ravioli—the pasta, the filling, all from scratch. We learn that real, official Parmesan cheese comes from Parma and the areas around it. Which makes perfect sense.

Then it's time for desserts. Oh boy. In less than an hour I know how to make chocolate mousse. Heavy cream, milk chocolate, and gelatin. I can do three-ingredient treats.

"Mom, this is awesome," I whisper as I lean closer to her. She's topping her mousse with sliced almonds. "Do you think we can do this more while we're in Italy this year? I kind of love it."

Mom continues to decorate her dessert with chocolate sauce. "Absolutely," she says. "I say we try classes in different places. Next should be making tortellini in Bologna or Modena. That's where they came from."

This is seriously fun. I'll be learning about cooking in the towns that actually invented these foods. I can barely stop myself from grabbing my notebook to write everything down, but my hands are a mess. I do my best to remember it all so I can take notes later.

The chef comes over and helps me and Mom plate our desserts. We dot the plate with chocolate sauce designs, and this time I absolutely can't resist grabbing my camera. I wash my hands and then take photos of the plate from every angle.

We've gotten to taste some things, but after a short break we'll be coming back for dinner. Our dinner that we made from scratch.

"What are we making tomorrow?" I ask the chef.

"Ah, tomorrow is a new day," he says. "We get to decide our own menus."

I'm pretty sure he's talking about food, but it sure feels like he's talking about my life.

THIRTY

Dear Ella,

Mom and I spent two days at this amazing
cooking school before heading back today. I'm
super tired, but there's not a chance I'm falling
asleep on the train. Mom and I have been
talking nonstop about what we learned, and
we planned a week's worth of meals for when
we get home. I hope you like Italian food.

Wait until you hear about this place!

"This was a lot of fun, Mom," I say. "Thanks." I
expect a smile from her, but this one is a bit devious. "What?"

Mom pauses for a minute. "I told the culinary school we'd be back," she says. "With friends."

Over the past month Mom has spent some time out with the people at the office, but I have no idea who she's talking about. "Marissa?" I ask.

"No," says Mom. "*Your* friends. Okay, listen, ever since you told me about your e-mails to Ella becoming your weekly column, I've been thinking it would be really fun to have Ella and her family come out to visit. Maybe in the fall."

It had never even occurred to me that friends would visit. I mean, it's not like we're in Ohio and it's a drive you can do in half a day. It's ITALY.

"For real?" I ask.

"Yes, I mean, maybe I shouldn't have gotten your hopes up," she says. "I mentioned it to Ella's mom yesterday, but she seemed to be up for it. I offered to fly them out for your birthday."

I jump out of my seat and hug my mom. I don't need to say a thing. She knows this is the best gift EVER.

I settle back down and lean my head on her shoulder. And somehow, I manage to fall asleep.

* * *

When we get back to the apartment, I get a text from Logan.

Did you see your post?!

We were so busy the last two days, I hadn't even thought to check. Marissa said she wanted to start the column "soon," but I didn't think she meant this soon.

No. Should I look? I text back.

He replies immediately. **Going to take a while to read the comments!**

Comments? I thought only Zara and Logan got a lot of comments. I open my laptop and go right to the blog. There it is: *Dear, Ella.*

I read through the whole thing, and even though I know what it says because I wrote it, it's like I'm reading someone else's words. Someone who's a writer. Someone who's pretty good at what she does.

When I get to the bottom, I sit back, then lean in again to make sure my eyes aren't playing tricks on me: *234 comments.*

Oh, come on. How is that even possible? I click on the link, and a whole page of responses pops up.

There are plenty of comments from people I

don't know, saying things like thank you, because that's how they felt when they moved away from home. One girl talks about the struggle between wanting to be somewhere else but so badly wanting to be home at the same time. They're having conversations. People are talking because I brought them together.

When I scroll down more, my heart pounds from the familiar names. Ella's comment simply says, *Way to go, Skyler!* Then there's Travis and a bunch of our other friends. They're having a conversation in the comments too.

How do people even know about this? I text Logan.

Zara and I spread the word on social media, he writes back. **Plus, the magazine promoted it on its website!**

"Mom, come here!" I shout. She runs in my room with a look that says she's not sure if something is wrong or really, really right.

"What is it, Skyler?" she asks.

"You have to see this," I say. "You won't believe it."

She sits next to me and scrolls through the comments. We read silently together for the next twenty minutes, and then she simply smiles.

"I did it," I say.

"You did it," she repeats. "I'm really proud of you."

It's not like she's never said those words before, but this might be the first time I've been one million percent certain she means them.

When she gets up to go in the other room, I call once more. "Mom?"

"Yes, honey?"

"I'm really excited about staying here," I say. "I'm happy for you. It's going to be a lot of fun."

Mom takes a slow breath, like she's relieved. "Would you like to go shopping tomorrow to get the new apartment ready?" she asks.

I nod. "Dad will love it here."

"You're the Venice expert now," she says. "You'll have to show him around."

She gives me a wink and leaves the room. It's quiet, and as the light outside starts to dim, the glowing screen of my laptop lights up the room.

THIRTY-ONE

'm surprised when I get a text early Thursday morning. It's from Zara.

Can we talk?

I don't even know how to respond, but I'm in too good of a mood to let her ruin it for me.

Sure. Where?

As soon as I hit send, there's a knock on the front door. Mom is already up and about, and the sound of muffled voices makes its way to my room.

Mom pops her head in. "Oh, good, you're up. You have a visitor."

I piece it together based on the text and the unsure look on Mom's face. I quickly change out of my pajamas and pull my hair back into a pony-tail.

Zara is sitting in the living room when I get there.

"Hi," I say, not knowing what else to add.

"Hi." She moves over on the couch, and I take it as a sign to sit down. Mom sneaks off to her room, probably to give us some privacy.

"You're wondering why I'm here," Zara begins.

Well, yeah. "A little bit," I say instead.

"I read 'Dear Ella,'" she says. "Your post was amazing."

Is she . . . complimenting me?

"Oh . . . thank you," I say. I wait, because it feels like she's going somewhere with this.

"I've never had an Ella." Zara grabs a pillow and moves it to her lap. "I can only imagine what it would be like to have a friend you can talk to like that."

Everything she's done runs through my mind, but the sad look in her eyes makes it all seem so unimportant right now.

"It must be hard to move around all the time," I say. "But I guess you have to with your parents' jobs, right?"

Zara takes a slow, deep breath. "It's not their

jobs," she says. "I *could* go with them, but they'd rather shuffle me from relative to relative."

It's more than she's told me about herself the whole time we've been here. I don't know whether to ask more questions or just let her talk.

"That's why you're with your aunt?" I decide to ask.

Zara nods. "Will you tell me about your friends?"

My first reaction is that this is a trick, but we're not competing anymore, so there's nothing for her to gain.

"Sure," I say. "But be warned. Some of them are pretty quirky."

Zara lets out a quick giggle. "I like quirky."

I pull out my phone and show her pics of my friends and tell her story after story. I even explain my bucket list challenge with Ella. It makes me miss home, but it also reminds me how lucky I am.

"I'm sorry, Skyler," she says when there's a break in conversation.

"For what?" I ask.

"For everything." Zara squeezes the pillow again. "I should have been nicer."

It's the apology I've been waiting for, except instead of making me feel better, it makes me realize something.

"I could have been nicer to you too," I say. "I guess I've just never met anyone like you. And you pushed me to do better. Even if it wasn't a very nice push."

We both laugh.

"Listen, I'm not saying I can be your Ella, but I can at least be your friend," I say. "If you're willing to give it a try."

"Yeah," she says. "I have the school-year internship and you've got your weekly column. We could work together." This time she doesn't give me her usual smirk; it's only three-quarters smirk and maybe one-quarter smile. I'll take it.

"If I didn't know better, I'd say you're a little bit happy for me." I return the three-quarter smirk.

"Happy is a bit of a stretch," says Zara. "I'm just glad the internships went to the most qualified candidates."

Ah, and now we're back to normal. I hate to admit it, but I think I'd miss the challenge if she suddenly started giving me credit instead of a hard time.

THIRTY—TWO

Dear Skyler,

When you get this from the mailbox,
I hope you'll be excited that you'll be
back in Italy soon.

You might not know exactly who you are
just yet or what the year will bring, but
listen to me and remember this . . . You
have plenty of time to figure it all out.

Enjoy every second of this adventure.
xoxo Skyler

It might be silly, but when I find a postcard with the exact view of Venice I saw on that first day here, I can't help but send it to myself.

It'll be like bringing a little bit of summer back home with me.

I know we'll be here all year, but I have one more thing I want to do before we head back to the States.

Marissa agrees to take the whole writing team—which now includes me—into Venice to Piazza San Marco. That's what the locals call St. Mark's Square, so I guess I better start calling it that too.

Mom says she wouldn't miss this for the world.

Marissa pays the guy in the little booth, and we all pile into the elevator at the *campanile* (aka the bell tower). They say it's always the best view of Venice, but at dusk it's even more amazing. So here we are at dusk, checking one last thing off the list.

When we get to the top of the tower, we see the signs not to touch the bells. I'm amazed by how enormous they are as we walk underneath all five of them.

The guide tells us about the campanile collapsing in 1902 (not something you want to hear when you're actually *in* the tower) and how it was rebuilt in the same spot. I walk to one side and, wow—the view.

The lagoon is in front of me, and the lights of the city line the water. Shiny reflections scatter all over. It's beautiful.

"Get some pictures," Mom reminds me.

Oh, right. It's like that first walk through the city when I was so amazed by everything. I forgot to take pictures then too.

Some of the gondolas are covered with blue tarps. They're done for the day. But other boats are out in the water, all lit up. The piazza in the front is still dotted with people as they walk around the two high columns.

To my right is the Doge's Palace (I still need to get there too!) and the start of the Grand Canal. As I walk around the tower, there's Piazza San Marco, where people and pigeons have learned to coexist. I think about the day Zara and I went on our spy mission there and ended up meeting Gino. It's more familiar now. Not just a temporary stop but *my* Venice.

The bells start ringing and it's pretty loud, so I cover up my ears until they stop.

"Good call on making this the last spot to see this summer," says Logan. "I can't believe *this* is where we're going to be all year." I stand beside him as we look out over the lagoon.

"And we get to write about it," I say. Logan and Zara smile like they know exactly what I mean. Writers need writer friends who understand.

"I'm glad we're all staying," says Zara. "It wouldn't be right if we'd been split up."

Marissa and Mom join us, and we all just stare out at the water.

I grab Mom's hand. Her fingers wrap around mine. "Stay connected," I accidentally think out loud.

"What, honey?" asks Mom.

"Oh, nothing," I answer. "I was just thinking about something Ella said."

Mom squeezes my hand. "This really is an incredible view of Venice," she says.

Her words seem to float through the air around us, and no one says a thing. Because sometimes, even if you're a real, official, I-have-my-own-column-now writer and you really want to write about how incredible the moment is . . . there simply are no words.

AUTHOR'S NOTE

In *Postcards from Venice,* Skyler struggles with the idea of figuring out what she's good at and what she'll do in the future, especially since everyone around her seems to know exactly what they want. It was important to me for Skyler to eventually discover that she doesn't have to have all the answers right now.

My mother once wrote about her experience with this as a child, and I think it's great advice, not only for the fictional Skyler, but also for my very real readers. Yes, practice and study to improve, but also remember to explore your interests, try new things, and learn as you go.

My mother was always there for me, encouraging me every step of the way. It's time your words were in a book too, Mom.

Excerpted from "The Past Revisited"
by Sandy Manel Predmore

I couldn't find it in any book. Page after page, I
leafed through a stack of magazines with only
one thought running through my mind—*I've
got to find a picture of what I want to be when I
grow up.*

Doesn't my teacher understand? I kept
thinking. *I don't know what I want to be, so how
can I find it in any magazine?*

I continued to turn the pages with the
pretense of searching, knowing all the while
that I wasn't going to find anything. It wasn't *in*
any book. It hadn't even been created in my
own mind yet. . . .

If I could return to that second-grade
classroom, I'd knock at the door and ask to
see Sandy Manel. As she'd make her way to
the other side of the room, the other children
would be whispering, "Who's that lady? Why
does she want to talk to Sandy?"

Immediately, upon gazing at my face, she'd
know who I was. Excitedly, she'd take me by
the hand, lead me to the front of the class

and proudly introduce me to her teacher and classmates. "I want you to see who I am when I'm grown up!"

Suddenly, a hushed stillness would permeate the room as everyone turned their undivided attention to us. They'd want to know all about me, and I'd tell them the many things I had done in my life. Sandy's reaction would be, "Wow. How exciting!"

After giving me a great big hug and thanking me for coming, she'd then rush to her desk and voraciously begin flipping through the pages of those same magazines once again, but this time with a renewed energy. She'd rip out pictures and words, then cut and paste until they were just what she wanted them to be. The result would be not just one picture, but a collage of many careers.

Satisfied with her finished project, she'd proudly hand it to her teacher and say, "Here, now it's ready to be put with the others. This is what I want to be when I grow up!"

ACKNOWLEDGMENTS

I took up five pages for acknowledgments in my last book, *No Place Like Home*, so I'm going to do my best to keep this one short. (Well, short*er*, anyway.)

As always, a huge thank-you to my editor, Alyson Heller and the team over at Aladdin. Alyson, gelato will be my treat if we take that work trip to Italy. Annabelle Metayer, you outdo yourself with each beautiful cover. To my agent, Uwe Stender, I hope you know how truly special you are, but just in case, I plan to keep telling you. Giddyup! Brent Taylor, I will thank you here for your enthusiasm and encouragement on our picture-book journey, and for being a genuinely wonderful person.

Thank you to my writer friends and writing

groups for always being so supportive. For this book specifically, thank you to Gail Nall, Janet Sumner Johnson, and Annie Sullivan for your reads and advice.

For letting me ask lots and lots of questions so I could make the details authentic, thank you to Alyssa Palombo, Nancy Eckerson, Robyn Harder, Kristen Sherman, and Elizabeth Dunn. Any errors are my own.

To my friends near and far, I love you, and I am so very grateful for your support and encouragement. FLGT Girls, when I write about true friendship, I think of us. To my friend-since-kindergarten Katie Bott, who I somehow managed to leave out of those aforementioned acknowledgments—thank you for always being there for me, and for making me laugh when I need it most. To Wendy, for your "dauntless resolution and unconquerable faith," and for always being by my side. Thank you to my travel companions for all our adventures—they continue to fill me with so many ideas for my stories. To my neighbors and their kids who are always willing to be my sounding board or film crew—thank you, Claire, Hailey, Bess, and Kate! Thank you, kid readers—Sage, Ishaani, Sahana, Madigan, Mallory, Abigail,

Scout, Norah, Maria, Sydney, Caitlin, Malaina, Grace, Madison, Lola, Miles, Brenna, Rebecca, Cate, and Madilynn!

To my Predmore and Manel families for your enthusiasm and support. Big thanks to my cousin Amie and Aunt Diane for all the fun launch party food. Yum. To my wonderful in-laws, Bonnie, Jack, Linda, Fred, Cathy, Karen, and the rest of our Canadian family, for always being so proud of me. For my mom, who surely would have been singing with the gondoliers if life had taken us to Venice. And for my dad, whose love of travel has definitely rubbed off on me—trips with you are some of my favorite memories.

Thank you to my kitties, Sienna and Smoky, who keep me company when I write. My husband, Rob, who never complains about the endless piles of books I bring home from the library. And my kids, Nathan and Kiley, who don't really care what I write here, because they just want to see their names in the book. I love you for being you.

Looking for another great book?
Find it
IN THE MIDDLE.

Fun, fantastic books for kids
in the in-be**TWEEN** age.

IntheMiddleBooks.com

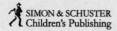